Women's Co-operative Printing Union

Healing Power of Mind

a treatise on mind-cure - with original views on the subject - and complete

instructions for practice, and self treatment

Women's Co-operative Printing Union

Healing Power of Mind
a treatise on mind-cure - with original views on the subject - and complete instructions for practice, and self treatment

ISBN/EAN: 9783337399627

Printed in Europe, USA, Canada, Australia, Japan

Cover: Foto ©Andreas Hilbeck / pixelio.de

More available books at **www.hansebooks.com**

HEALING POWER OF MIND.

A TREATISE ON MIND-CURE, WITH ORIGINAL VIEWS ON
THE SUBJECT, AND COMPLETE INSTRUCTIONS FOR
PRACTICE, AND SELF-TREATMENT.

BY

JULIA ANDERSON ROOT.

"Man is the greatest fact in Nature,
Mind is the greatest fact in Man."

SAN FRANCISCO:
WOMEN'S CO-OPERATIVE PRINTING OFFICE, 424 MONTGOMERY STREET.
1884.

PREFACE.

The mind-cure is just now exciting a great deal of public interest. Within these last few years several books have been published on the subject, and we have decided to add to the number. Our reasons for doing so are, that we hold some views different from any that have hitherto been printed, and, further, we wish to place before readers certain facts and principles that will enable them to successfully treat themselves. We have given several chapters on subjects that have a bearing upon, and are intimately related to, mental healing. These chapters are intended in some instances to be more suggestive than exhaustive, but we are nevertheless led to believe that they will in all cases prove instructive.

"Mental healing," "mind-cure," "metaphysical science," or by whatever name it may be known, is not a new system. In all ages of the world there have been persons who have cured diseases that learned medical practitioners have pronounced incurable. These cases have been effected by the power of mind, and we are confident from our own experience, that the more this invisible agent is brought to bear upon the human system, the less sickness and suffering we shall have in the world. We expect the aid and co-operation of our churches, irrespective of sect, and, in fact, of good and intelligent people everywhere, in our efforts to lessen the sum of human misery and woe. It is sad to see the lives of so many of God's children embittered by disease, when the remedy lies in their own hands. Each and all can do something towards remedying this state of things. Our efforts we feel will be crowned with at least as much success in the future as they have been in the past.

JULIA ANDERSON ROOT.

San Francisco,
    August 1st, 1884.

CONTENTS.

INSTRUCTIONS FOR HEALING.

PROGRESS.

EDUCATION OF MOTHERS.

SPIRITUALISM.

ANTIQUITY OF MIND CURE.

EFFICACY OF PRAYER.

PERSONAL EXPERIENCE.

INSANITY.

NECESSITY OF CONDITIONS.

QUESTIONS AND ANSWERS.

INTRODUCTION.

Physical courage is common enough the world over. Man, whether savage, semi-civilized or intelligent, shows himself to be possessed of powers that defy physical pain and despise death. The histories of all wars, whether amongst the barbarians or the enlightened nations, are full of deeds of heroism. But, the man that will beard the lion in his den—face the tiger in the jungles, and march to the cannon's mouth without flinching, will yet tremble at the breath of public opinion—will blanch at the attack of a scurrilous newspaper, and be turned from the path of duty by a little opposition and ridicule. Physical courage is common both to man and beast, but moral courage is a plant of rarer growth. And while we hear a great deal about the wants of the age, we say that the great want of the age is that very moral courage which, in spite of all bitterness and opposition, contempt and contumely, will dare to adhere to the true and the good. The great desire of most men is to be thought, or to seem to be, good and true, without much caring whether or not they possess these qualities. Public approbation and applause may be good things in their way, but the time comes in the lives of all men when they are called upon to think in certain directions and to perform certain acts that run counter to popular knowledge and prejudice, and which are sure for a time to bring them an amount of public condemnation and ridicule. This book is published in the interests of the health of humanity, and we cannot but expect that amongst a certain class that our efforts will be received with disfavor and opposition. We refer of course to the medical practitioners. We shall certainly not say worse of this class than they say of themselves. But the fault we find with medical men as a class is, that they speak and act as if they had a monopoly of diseases and their cures. They think and act in certain grooves, and woe be to the man who dares to depart from their established methods. This fact is written all down the history of the practice of medicine. Every advanced thinker in their own ranks has been persecuted in every conceivable manner. Harvey, Jenner, Simpson, Elliotson, and a host of others who have made advanced steps have been pounced upon by the whole fraternity and characterized as innovators and madmen. Who does not remember the fierce and bitter opposition that awaited the man who discovered chloroform? Even preachers from the pulpit denounced the employment of that anæsthetic as flying in the face of the Almighty, who according to their notions, had ordained that man should feel the pain attending upon the amputation of a limb. We could multiply these cases *ad infinitum*, as the schoolmen would say. But our object is to call attention to the fact that no man, and no class of men—dignify themselves by what titles they may—can say to the advancing waves of knowledge, thus far shalt thou come and no further. True knowledge cometh from God, and it is no man's and no set of men's exclusive property. And when men can be brought to recognize this great fact, and act upon it, then will the world come to rejoice in true progression. As the matter at present stands most people allow certain privileged classes to do their thinking for them, and as a consequence we are surrounded by an atmosphere of mental and moral slavery. More particularly is this true of diseases and their remedies. Now, we want the moral courage that will dare to cut aloof from these old medical traditions, and take this matter of health and disease into our own hands.

Is it not time that something should be done in this direction? The flood-gates of disease are open and the whole army of medical practitioners are powerless to stem the tide. Archimedes is reported to have said, "Give me a lever long enough and a fulcrum strong enough, and I will move the world." We say, give us the truth of metaphysical science and the courage to apply it, and we will lift from off humanity the mountains of disease that have so long oppressed them. How simple is truth and its application, when its principles are known. The old Romans, at immense expense and labor, built huge aqueducts over hill and valley. But the necessity of these costly labors was entirely done away with by a knowledge that water would rise to the level of its source.

But, to return to the subject of intellectual daring, "God," says Luther, "does not have his work made manifest by cowards." All the blessings that we enjoy under the names of civil and religious liberty, all the improvements that have taken place in science, have sprung from the small minority of daring and advanced thinkers. It is sad to think how large a number of men do their thinking by proxy, which is the same as saying they do not think at all. And yet God requires of every man that he shall exercise the powers of his own mind, and without he does this, he lives in mental slavery, which is, after all, a more degrading position than physical bondage. Let a man stand proudly and grandly before the material things of this universe, and not regard himself as an interloper in a world where he deems matter everything and himself nothing. It is mind that is everything, and before its powers matter is as nothing. It is this great truth that we have endeavored to set forth in the following pages.

GOD AND CREATION.

Creation! What a stupendous word! What does it mean? Who can interpret it to us so that our intellect shall be fed and satisfied with the explanation? Many learned and philosophical treatises have been written on this subject, but we venture to assert that but few authors, either ancient or modern, have advanced the human mind one step in this direction. Why is this? We answer, that it is because they have started on a wrong basis; their questions have been asked in the wrong direction. They have ransacked the rocks; they have sounded the depths of old ocean; delved to the very bowels of the earth; laid bare the fossil remains of bygone ages, and showed us the footprints of all the early forms of life, from the inconceivably small insect to the huge monster that dwelt in the primeval forest; and yet, after all these researches, the human mind still asks "What is creation? Had it a beginning? Can it have an ending?" "All things from a clam!" exclaimed the elder Darwin. But how did he know that a clam or anything else was the beginning of life even on this earth, to say nothing of other planets and worlds and suns that everywhere roll on in the boundless fields of ether? Says the divine Herschel, "Who shall tell what countless forms of life sleep beneath earth's granite pavements?" And yet, most geologists assume to trace all forms of life as coming into existence after the laying down and formation of granite. But suppose, that if instead of aiming to wring the secrets of God and creation from visible and external nature, that we turn to the invisible and internal; suppose we try the realm of mind and turn away from the realm of matter.

The idea of creation implies a creator; and according to the popular notion, there was a time when this creator began to create; which would mean that there was a time when the Almighty world-builder was idle. The Bible, reason, intuition, all forbid such a conclusion. We are told that God is the same to-day, yesterday and forever; and He, accordingly, was always a creator, and has from all eternity been creating. This we affirm is the only conclusion we can arrive at; it is the only satisfactory stand that we can take in dealing with this subject. That this world had a beginning is undoubtedly true; but what is true of this earth cannot be true of an eternal universe that had no beginning. If we expect to fully understand this, we expect too much from the finite intellect; but there are some things which we cannot understand and yet are com-

pelled to believe. For instance, who can understand
infinite space, and yet we are compelled to believe in
its infinitude. We can conceive of no boundary ; in
other words, we cannot conceive of any obstruction in
space where there is not something beyond. We
believe in infinity of time and space because it is a law
of mind that compels us so to believe. The cause of
this belief comes from the invisible mind and not from
visible matter. Now, we apply the same process of
reasoning, or rather of intuition, to God and creation.
No man by searching—that is, searching in the
realms of visible matter—can find out God ; but we can
get perceptions or conceptions of Him by trusting to
what we shall call, for the want of better terms, the
instincts of our invisible soul. So that as we are compelled to believe that time and space are eternal, so we
are compelled to believe that God and creation are
eternal also.

All mythologies are full of ingenious endeavors to
account for the beginning of creation. These attempts
have been no more reasonable then are the endeavors
to account for the origin of time and space. How can
that, which from its very nature is eternal, have a
beginning ? The idea is absurd and preposterous.
Amongst the early Hindoos everything was supposed
to be hatched from an egg. But where did the egg
come from ? It will be seen that these people reasoned

from the known phenomena of nature to account for the origin of nature itself.   As the egg from a chicken produces a chicken, so in their minds creation and even God Himself were hatched into being.   Not only have these attempts been made to account for God's exist-ence by a material process, but millions of persons, even in Christian lands, want to know of God through their material senses.   They want to hear, touch and see God the same as they can the mortal frame of a man—God is a spirit and as such must be thought of and approached.   The idea that God is a person and has parts like a man belongs to a pagan age.   When we say God is not a person like a man, we do not thereby deny that he has no personality whatever. We have no desire in this connection to fly to a dic-tionary for a definition of the word person, for that would limit our meaning.   Locke somewhere says, that "a person is a thinking, intelligent being."   We mean that God is a person in that He is distinct from nature, and is the eternal, intelligent and active principle of all creation—and that as He is eternal so is creation co-eternal with God.   Newton, the great Christian philosopher, says, that God is all eye, all arm, all ear. Of course these expressions are simply intended to convey to us that God is everywhere, and that he is all powerful to execute His own will.   A poet writes :

" When by the wind the tree is shaken,
    There's not a bough or leaf can fall,
But of its falling heed is taken
    By One who sees and governs all.

The tree may fall and be forgotten,
    And buried in the earth remain,
Yet from its juices, rank and rotten,
    Springs vegetating life again.

The world is with creation teeming,
    And nothing ever wholly dies,
And things that are destroyed in seeming,
    In other shapes and forms arise.

And nature still unfolds the tissue
    Of unseen work by Spirit wrought,
And not a work but hath its issue
    With blessing or with evil fraught."

With regard to the creation of man we are told in Genesis, 1, 26 and 27 :

"And God said, Let us make man in our own image, after our likeness : and let them have dominion over the fish of the sea, and over the fowl of the air, and over the cattle, and over all the earth, and over every creeping thing that creepeth upon the earth.

So God created man in his own image, in the image of God created he him : male and female created he them."

We must put a reasonable and intelligent construction upon these sentences. Man cannot be made in the image and likeness of God in power and intelligence. The finite cannot be like the infinite. God is not limited in knowledge and goodness, but man is. But man may be like unto God in the essence of his being, because he is a spark 'of the celestial fire. A drop of water is, chemically speaking, in the image and likeness of the whole ocean, but it has not the powers of the whole ocean, for the latter can roll mighty waves—raise storms and bear ships on its bosom. In a broad and grand sense the drop is not like the ocean. And though man is in one sense the image and likeness of God, yet he is not like God in all things, for He has infinite and eternal powers not possessed by man. Nevertheless, this divine likenesss, or if we may so call it, this divine kinship, should awaken in the breast of every man a conscious grandeur of his divine origin and mission. It was in a moment of inspiration that a poet transported himself to the starry worlds above and exclaimed,—

> '"Even here, I feel
> Among these mighty things, that as I am
> I am akin to God ; that I am part
> Of the use universal, and can grasp
> Some portion of that reason in the which
> The whole is ruled and founded, and that I have
> A spirit nobler in its cause and end,
> Lovelier in order, greater in power,
> Than all these bright and swift immensities."

Still, though man should grandly feel the majesty of his own existence, yet when he contemplates God and creation he will feel his own littleness.   He will feel his vast ignorance in the presence of this vast intelligence.

> " The Lord of all, Himself through all diffused,
> Sustains, and is the life of all that lives,
> Nature is but a name for an effect,
> Whose cause is God."

THE ORIGIN OF EVIL.

The account of the origin of evil as recorded in the book of Genesis is not accepted literally by intelligent Christians of the present day. Philosophers have exercised their thought and ingenuity in endeavoring to solve this great problem, and yet to-day it remains as great a mystery as ever. Pope says—

> " All nature is but art unknown to thee;
> All chance, direction which thou canst not see;
> All discord, harmony not understood;
> All partial evil, universal good."

After all, this is an unsatisfactory explanation. It is simply an admission of evil and an assertion that it is good. From whatever standpoint we view nature, we find that a system of dualism prevails through all her works. There are light and darkness, heat and cold, attraction and repulsion, upper and under, inner and outer, and good and evil. Whatever name we call evil by, whether ignorance, or as some doubtful philosophers term it, "undeveloped good," it is still our enemy in whatever shape it appears. To destroy it is our duty, and that of everyone on earth. Make heat, and the cold is banished; kindle a light, and the darkness dis-

perses of itself; let in the rays of truth and science upon
disease, and it will flee away.   Most theologians start
with the assertion that there are two great powers in
the universe, a God who is powerful for all good, and a
Devil who is powerful for all evil, and that these
powers are co-existent and co-eternal, and have been
warring against each other through all eternity for
supremacy.   We have admitted the personality of God,
but we deny the personality of a Devil. Discord, error,
sin, sickness, ignorance and irreverence are the devils
that mislead and torment us.   We let in upon these the
light of God's truth.   We fight disease with the weapons which He has placed in the minds of all His
children, and we can become conquerors.

Who has not read Milton's Paradise Lost?   This
grand old man in his blindness, conceived the idea
that he could "in the height of his great argument
justify the ways of God to man."   According to his
idea, evil commenced when some archangels in heaven
began a war against their maker.   They and their
adherents were overthrown in that war and were cast
out of heaven.   But does this idea settle the question?
Does it account for the origin of evil?   Let us see.
Like produces like.   The beginning of every action is
a thought—a thought good or bad is the seed of an
action—and it will at once be seen that no rebellious
action could have taken place without being preceded

by rebellious thoughts or designs. Whence came those evil thoughts ? They had their origin in something. They could not have an origin in goodness. Let no reader be startled when we assert that evil or discord or sin, or by whatever name we call it, is one of the necessities of creation. This we submit is the doctrine taught by Christ. In Mat., 18:7, it is said, "Wo unto the world because of offences, for it must needs be that offences come; but wo to that man by whom the offence cometh." Why must it needs be? Simply because it is a necessity, and this necessity is perfectly compatible with the good and righteous government of God. God is a creator, but He cannot create a being equal to Himself, all that He creates must be beneath Himself in intelligence and in power, which is the same as saying that we are limited or finite beings. Being thus limited, man must necessarily err, and from this error comes sin and suffering. This is the way, in the face of all the learned treatises on philosophy and theology, that we account for the existence of the suffering and misery of the world.

Now, let us turn to the other side of the picture. Man is made after the image of God ; he is a spark of the divine essence ; he possesses within himself the power to conquer error; to subdue disease and turn discord to harmony. Thus far we have shown the reasonableness, the justice and goodness of the creation. But when we say that man is made after the image of God, we do not mean physically. When we affirm that man is made after the likeness of God, we do not mean alike in power, in intelligence and goodness, but in likeness in having a part of his nature, in having a soul that is divine in its essence. But as this soul in him must, as we have before seen, from the necessities of creation be limited in its powers, it cannot grasp all knowledge ; it must commit errors, and thus originates sin and sickness. The objection here that can be made is this : If God has created man so that he must trangress, is it just that he should be punished for his transgression ? We answer, perfectly so, because it is a necessity.

And we speak reverently ; there are necessities that surround God himself ; in other words there are impossibilities even to the Great Creator. We need here only again refer to the impossibility of God creating a being equal to Himself. He alone is perfectly good, and He cannot create the perfectly good, but while He cannot do this He can and has created beings capable of continually striving after goodness and intelligence. This necessitates a man having a will and a power of selection for his needs, wants and progress. When he does not so select he does not fulfill the needs of his soul in its path of progression, and the result is pain. This pain is necessary and just, for without this reminder man would not strive to unfold his being and fulfil his part in the great plan of his Creator.

Now, if there are necessities that surround even God Himself in creation, much more so are there necessities that surround man in his life. The laws of God are no respecters of persons. They are like Himself eternal and unchangeable. It is a necessity that they must punish all violations, whether they are made knowingly or unknowingly. A law to be a law must be constant and undeviating under all circumstances. It is not possible to conceive it otherwise. Who can imagine a law of gravitation determining in itself when it shall punish and when it shall not punish? Who can imagine a power in the sea to say when man shall or shall not drown in it?

Whoever a man may be, saint or savage, pope or peasant, or whether he falls into the water accidentally or plunges into it with suicidal intent if he remains under water a sufficient length of time the result will be death. That is a necessity of law and creation.

MIND AND MATTER.

Much has been written on these subjects, and we shall touch upon them only so far as they have a strict relation to the purposes of this work. Byron wrote :

"When Berkeley said there was no matter and proved it
No matter what he said."

This might have been intended as a witticism, but it is certainly no reply to the position taken by the great philosopher. Berkeley is not alone in his views upon this subject, for philosophers in all ages have endeavored to show to those who claimed that this universe was nothing but a workshop, wherein all the changes we witness are but the results of the chemical play of atoms, that after all they knew nothing about it, or at least made claims for it that neither fact nor reason would warrant them in doing. What matter really is has never been defined. We only know of it by certain properties, such as form, size, weight, color and so forth. These properties whether taken individually or collectively are not matter itself, but only certain properties of a something that we call matter. Color is but the color of something—size is only the size of something—and so it can be said of all the other properties ; but these are not the thing itself. Is there anything underlying all these properties ? If so, we do not know what that something is. How do we become conscious of those properties? It is only through our sense of sight and touch and the obstruction we meet with in matter that we become conscious of any existence. In other words, as we know of matter by properties, the recognition of those properties entirely depends upon senses or the quality of mind. Let us illustrate this still further. There is a something that we call pain. Let a person be pricked with a needle, the result will be pain. What makes that result. Certainly not the needle.

The steel of which it is composed could feel no pain. What felt the pain ? Every physicist will at once say that it was the nerve that felt the pain—and without the existence of a nerve there could be no such thing as pain. We speak of a burn from the fire producing pain ; but if there were no nerves to feel, there could be no sensation of pain from the burn. Again, there is another thing that we call sound. How is this made up ? Take a small bell and ring it. The tongue strikes against the side of the bell causing it to vibrate. These vibrations set the air in motion, producing in it a wave-like motion, and when these waves fall upon the ear, they produce a result we call sound. But if there was no ear to catch those waves there could be no such result as sound. What we have said of feeling and hearing can be applied with equal force of reasoning to all the other senses. But we must go one step further back. When we speak of the nerves of sight, of hearing, of smell and so forth, we by no means wish to imply that it is these material nerves that in themselves perform the functions attributed to them. On the other hand we contend that it is not the eye that sees nor the ear that hears. The eye is but the instrument which conveys impressions to the invisible mind. In itself it has no more the power to see than has the telescope or microscope. Look at a human body when the life has departed from it. All the organs are there —the nerves are still in existence, but there is no sensation, and the body, whether you dissect it or burn it, can suffer no pain. And why? Because the invisible power that felt, that saw, heard and performed all the other powers, has departed. So that we are driven to the conclusion that matter, in itself, has no intelligence nor feeling, and does not possess even the power of motion. Thus, if we raise an arm and ask the physicist or materialist by what power we perform the act, he readily answers that it is merely muscular motion. If we ask further, what moved the muscles? He replies, the nerves. What then moved the nerves? He answers, the brain. We further desire to know

what moved the brain ?   Here we answer for him and
say it is the spirit.   Brain is not the organ of mind in
the same sense that the liver is the organ of hepatic
secretion.   Brain is the organ of *the* mind.   It does not
produce mind, but is acted upon by it.   The body does
not produce life, but is acted upon and vivified by it.
Take a seed of any description, analyse it, subject it to
any chemical test you please, can you tell or point out
its principle of life ?   No ! this is invisible, and yet it
is that invisible power in it that is the all-important
thing.   Turn which way we will, it is the invisible that
acts upon, that governs, animates and moves dead visible matter.   And we know of no limit that the invisible
mind, when used under the powers of science, has over
matter.   In one sense we may call it all-powerful.

But if we know little about the nature of matter, so
also do we know but little about the nature of mind.
We know nothing of its essence, we only know of it
by its powers and effects, and of these we are in the
main ignorant.   How wonderful even is memory.   By
what process are words, ideas and scenes impressed
upon and retained in the mind?   Every mind is one
vast picture gallery upon which is photographed all
that we have seen, learned, suffered and enjoyed.
Not always to be called up by our own volition, and
not always present to our consciousness.   A landscape,
a verse, a quotation, may slumber in the mind for long,

long years without being remembered, when suddenly some trifling thing will call up from the chambers of sleep the forgotten impression. Then the effect of mind upon mind is equally mysterious. How often are our thoughts and feelings projected into the mind of another without our own intention or knowledge. How grand and yet how silent is this power of mind exercised ; there is no beating of drums, no blowing of trumpets, no sounding of gongs, no booming of cannon, and yet the effects of this silent power and march of mind are greater, grander, than the tramp of armed millions and the thunder of all the artillery in the world. The noise, the pomp, the power of the one shall pass away, but the other shall endure forever.

There is one other attribute of mind that we must notice, and that is its power to endow matter with the power of sensation, and enabling it to receive impressions. These impressions may become beliefs. But these sensations, impressions, and beliefs, are not eternally lasting, but like the matter which they are impressed upon, can be removed and dissolved. Thus, it will be seen, that we make mind to have a two-fold existence. But we give these two states two different names. The soul pure and simple we call the "immortal mind." The other condition which is produced by the influence of mind upon matter we call the "mortal mind." In all investigations in the science of metaphysical healing, it is important to bear these distinctions in mind. Let it be understood that though we say "mortal mind," we do not wish the reader to infer that this condition will necessarily pass away at the change called death. These impressions and conditions if not conquered in this life, will have to be destroyed in the next sphere of existence by our own volition. How important then it is for our own happiness here and hereafter to live according to the spiritual laws of God.

THINGS SEEN AND UNSEEN.

It is commonly said of the Egotist—"he thinks he knows it all, and what he does not know is not worth knowing." It may be affirmed more forcibly that men generally think they see it all, and that what they do not see is not worth seeing. There is no sense, no power of the mind, that men are tyrannized over so much as by their eyesight, They are, in fact, to a very large extent, the slaves of their vision. St. Paul says : "The things which are seen are temporal, but the things which are unseen are eternal." He doubtless had strict reference to spiritual things as distinguished from things material. But we desire for a moment to call attention to the things which physicists class as natural phenomena. All the mighty forces of nature are unseen. And yet how rarely men think of these things. We gaze upon the locomotive as it speeds with its train of cars over hill and valley, without for a moment thinking that this power is derived from an unseen agent. The steam in the steam-chest is as invisible as the atmosphere we breathe. It is only when this steam comes in contact with the atmosphere and becomes

condensed, that it is visible. Men speak of the laws of
nature as if they were things that they could see and
handle. Whoever saw the law of gravitation or any
other law? And yet it is these invisible laws that
make and govern all the mighty and varied operations
which are ever taking place around us. The falling
apple, the crumbling mountain, the moving avalanche,
the roaring cataract, the rushing river, the raindrop,
the snowflake, all move and fall in obedience to this
invisible force of gravitation. We gaze upon a forest
of oaks and admire their towering strength as they
sway their strong arms in the blast. A fire will in a
few hours sweep that forest forever from our sight.
What survives? It is the invisible that survives and
again builds up the visible. The forest is gone, but we
have an acorn, and that acorn is capable of producing an
oak and a forest or a million of forests. The acorn is
visible it is true, but it is not its visible parts that perpetuate the oak. The germ, the life that sends out roots
and fibres, and trunks and branches, is an invisible something which we call life; and without this invisible something survived we could have no visible oaks. We can
see a wire of the electric telegraph, and the batteries,
and the operators at their instruments, but the power
that enables us to send words and messages over conti-
nents and through seas is invisible. Electricity is invisible, but it exists in and around every particle of matter,

animate and inanimate.   Take a common magnet and
hold it in close proximity to a needle, the needle is
drawn to it by a force ; but because we cannot see that
force, shall we say that it is of any less importance
than the needle and the magnet which we can see ?

How few persons realize that even as regards the
forms of life in the animal and vegetable kingdom, that
by far the greater number of varieties are not discernible
by the naked eye. There are living things "to whom the
fragile blade of grass, that springeth in the morn and
perisheth ere noon, is an unbounded world."   It has
been calculated that there are millions and millions of
insects in a cubic inch of water ; they are so small,
when compared with the finest grain of sand, that it is
impossible for us to conceive how they can possess
organs which enable them to pass and repass and
avoid each other; and yet they do these things, and
they show us that they have their likes and antipathies
the same as the animals which are our everyday
companions.

Again, our thought is often required to correct the
conclusion of our sight. It is not by our eyes alone that
we know the earth moves. We ascertain this fact by
the exercise of thought.   Mere vision would lead us to
come to exactly the opposite conclusion. So that, view
this universe in what aspect we please, we conclude,
first, that with regard to the so-called material things,

that it is the invisible mind that corrects and properly informs our sense ; next, that of all things in the universe it is the unseen which has power, that moulds and fashions the things which are seen, and that it alone endures forever. And when men shall fully understand and believe these things, that belief shall be to them as a new Messiah, purifying and regenerating their nature ; and then, in the fullness of joy, man will exclaim " I am one with God !"

MAN'S RELATION TO GOD AND CREATION.

The questions that follow next in order are these : What relation does man stand to creation and its creator ? What influence can he have over the world around ? To what extent can he make or mar his joys and sorrows ? Macaulay somewhere says, that touching the ways of God with man, the ignorant savage is as wise as the most learned philosopher. This may be true as a matter of reason ; but it is untrue as a matter of faith and intuition. But in order to let these faiths and intuitions have full play, man must throw aside his intellectual pride. It is this ingredient that has led him into the grand error of believing that all things were made purposely and solely for his use. A well known satirist writes :

> "Has God, thou fool ! worked solely for thy good,
> Thy joy, thy pastime, thy attire, thy food ?
> Who for thy table feeds the wanton fawn,
> For him has kindly spread the flowery lawn ;
> Is it for thee the lark ascends and sings ?
> Joy tunes his voice, joy elevates his wings.
> Is it for thee the linnet pours his throat ?
> Loves of his own, and raptures swell the note.

The bounding steed you pompously bestride
Shares with his lord the pleasure and the pride.
Is thine alone the seed that strews the plain ?
The birds of heaven shall vindicate their grain,
Thine the full harvest of the golden year ?
Part pays, and justly, the deserving steer ;
The hog, that ploughs not, nor obeys thy call,
Lives on the labors of this lord of all.
    Know, Nature's children all divide her care,
The fur that warms a monarch, warms a bear.
While man exclaims ' See all things for my use !'
' See man for mine !' replies a pampered goose.
And just as short of reason he must fall,
Who thinks all made for ne, onot one for all."

The poet Gray, in his immortal elegy, written in a country churchyard, too anxious to point a moral or adorn a tale, uses a false illustration when he writes :

"Full many a gem of purest ray serene
The dark unfathomed caves of ocean bear ;
Full many a flower is born to blush unseen,
And waste its sweetness on the desert air."

These lines, which have so often done duty in the pulpit, on the platform, and, in fact, in all the walks of literature and oratory, are a striking example of that intellectual pride and human conceit to which we have called attention. At the moment we write, there are countless myriads of the most gorgeous flowers of the most delicate hue and the choicest perfume, growing and blossoming in a thousand nooks and dells, and where they grow blossom and display a beauty beyond the power of man to imitate, there they die and find

no record in the brain of man, and their history is recorded in no book.   But shall we say that because
they thus live and die that their perfume, their beauty,
and use are wasted ?   This would indeed be telling God
that he has made things in vain, because they were not
intimately and immediately related to man and his con-
venience and comfort.   Because all the rays of sunlight
do not fall upon man and the little patch of ground that
he cultivates, shall we say that therefore those rays are
wasted ?   Unquestionably, every ray of light that falls
from yonder sun, whether falling upon the barren rock,
the sterile desert or the "dark unfathomed caves of
ocean," has its use and mission.   Are there not countless forms of vegetable and animal life in the depths of
the ocean, ay, in every drop of water, that require the
nourishing rays of light to preserve and perpetuate
their existence ?   " All things that on the earth do
dwell, unto the earth some special good do give."   The
grain of sand, the blade of grass, the tiny insect, the
towering mountain, the rolling river and the sounding
sea, are as much a necessary part of creation as man.
"All are but parts of one stupendous whole."   And when
man comes to recognize this great fact, then will he
come to look at things with an eye of faith, and not as
now, through the lens of a proud and utilitarian reason.
We should not stand with arrogance before this mighty
creation that everywhere encircles us, but with humility

and faith, and then things that are now dark to us will appear bright as the noonday. We should gaze upon this kingdom of God with the single-mindedness of a child. Christ says, "Whosoever shall not receive the kingdom of God as a little child, shall in no wise enter therein." If we approach God's works as if we knew all their mysteries then we shall know but little, but if we will sit down before them in humility and reverence then we shall learn more and more of His ways and shall be enabled to enter into the kingdom of His mysteries and power.

How far can man control and have power over and use the works of God? There are some things that are inexorable, that exist in spite of and cannot be controlled by the mind of man. There are the movements of the heavenly bodies, these are exact and are founded upon the principles of divine mathematics. There are also other things over which he cannot from their very nature exercise the slightest influence or control. He cannot destroy God's laws, but he can obey them and use them for his own happiness and progress. It is in this sense that God has given him dominion over all things around him. By the exercise of what power? By the power of mind. This power is the divinity in man. When it is told us that God made man after his own image we take it to mean that he made the spirit of man after his own essence.

Jesus taught this doctrine, He proclaimed that God acted through Him, that God spake through Him and that if we wanted to see God that we could do so in Him, and in ourselves when we thought and believed as He did. Thus we have presented to us " the golden key which opes the Palace of Eternity." Christ walked the wave, made the loaves and fishes, healed the sick and raised the dead. On what principles did He do these things? He himself tells us, that His power was from *God.* He never spake of disease as difficult or dangerous. He never employed drugs of any description. In fact, He in all cases implied that the cure for these diseases was not to be found in visible matter, but in invisible mind. When his followers brought to Him cases they could not heal, He said unto them, "Oh, ye of little faith." This age seems to have lost the meaning of the grandest and sublimest word in the English, or any other language, namely, FAITH. When St. Paul said "faith is the substance of things hoped for—the evidence of things not seen," he did not intend to give a complete definition of that word. Whenever Christ used the word faith, He evidently gave to it a meaning and power that were more potent for good than that possessed by all the other human powers combined. He spoke of faith as a law of God, as real in its operation as the law of gravitation or any other law by which this universe is guided and governed.

The question will arise in the minds of some persons as to the possibility of people in modern days possessing the power of affecting cures upon the same method as that recorded in Scripture. We answer this question from two standpoints. First, we take the words of Christ himself, who promised his followers, " The works that I do ye shall do." Next, we answer the question from the standpoint of fact, from which there can be. no escape for the caviler or the skeptic. We take our stand upon the doctrine, " by their fruits shall ye know them," so that from whatever point we consider the relation of man to God and creation—however we may view man as a being of power and duties in this sphere of existence—we are warranted in coming to the conclusion, that it is through mind, and faith in its unlimited powers, that he can conquer all disease and suffering, and error, that affect him in his journey through life.

THE MISSION AND·DUTY OF MAN.

Such of our readers as have perused Pope's Essay on Man, will agree with us that while that production stands unrivalled as a work of its kind, yet that it fails to satisfy either the head or heart. The work is entirely of a materialistic kind. Though here and there are to be found passages that appear to have their birth in the spiritual powers of our nature, yet the author seems to think that he could solve the problem of life, by reference to the visible world as judged of by the reasoning faculties of man. Viewed in this light the work is a splendid failure. What help does it give us to be told to

> " Laugh where we must, be candid where we can,
> But vindicate the ways of God to man.
> Say first of God above or man below,
> What can we reason, but from what we know.
> Of man, what see we but his station here,
> From which to reason or to which refer
> Through worlds unnumbered though the God be known,
> 'Tis ours to trace him only in our own."

We have elsewhere in this work aimed to show that man cannot solve those mighty problems that relate to existence by an appeal to reason, nor by consulting material nature. Here, again, we must refer to the intuitions and to faith. Man questions himself. What is the meaning of existence? Why am I here? What use am I to this universe? We affirm that there dwells, deep down in the bosom of every man, a belief that he comes into the world to do some work which no other man can do—a work imposed upon him by the very laws of his own being. This, to him, is an intuition. He cannot find the corroboration of this in the material universe, for his modicum of work seems to be swallowed up, and the only benefit he can witness is, that his labor enables him to clothe himself and procure food. If, perchance, he is enabled to lay aside a few pieces of yellow metal, yet the reflection will sometimes come, "Of what use can this be to me, I must soon pass away from earth, and as I cannot carry these things with me, of what use are they to me?" And still the question comes—to what end have I lived? Let us here try to explain and to illustrate. Man, we have seen, is but a part of "one stupendous whole." In other words, he is but one of the products of the great intelligent force that lies behind and produces and moves the whole universe. A grain of sand, a blade of grass, a pine tree, a mountain, could with as much reason assume to judge of the meaning of their existence as man. We, in common with all things, animate and inanimate, are alike products of the divine intelligence. Can the clay judge the potter? Have we not the right to presume, and is it not our reasonable duty to presume, that the power that produces and fashions us and all things knows more than ourselves? That power, we are assured, is not malignant. It could not have sent us into existence to punish us—for in this case it would have been better that we, and all things, should not have existed. Why is it that we have in our own nature a something that we call conscience, that approves what is right and condemns what is wrong? Why are we, in spite of ourselves, compelled to condemn cruelty, untruth and injustice? Simply, because we have something of the god-like within us. We all feel that the thing that is false and unjust must pass away. There is no man so low down, there is no soul stained so foully with sin but is compelled to love the good, the beautiful and true, and hate that which is false.

> " The darkest night that shrouds the sky
>   Of beauty hath a share ;
> The blackest heart has signs to tell,
>   That God still lingers there. "

From what we have here advanced we conclude that the universe is founded on immutable justice, and no man can successfully fight against that justice. Sooner or later that which is untrue and unjust must pass away.

> " And thus the world goes round and round,
>   And the genial seasons run,
> And ever the truth comes uppermost
>   And ever is justice done. "

Now, this power behind nature being just, and possessing an intelligence so far beyond that of the wisest of mortals that we cannot even conceive of its immensity, has not made anything in vain.   Our intelligence, glorified by faith, assures us that we are in this life for a purpose—that we are in fact workmen placed here to carry out the wise and beneficent plan of God.   An architect plans a temple, and his specifications are only so many directions to workmen what they are to do for its erection.   He says to one man, make this foundation ; to another, build these walls ; to a third, carve that image ; to a fourth, construct that roof.   And thus he places his workmen in the various positions where they can be useful.   But any of these workmen might say, "Of what use is my work ?   I can see no good, no use in it.   It is incomplete in itself and must end in nothing."   But the architect who placed these men at their different tasks, knew that if every man faithfully performed his own work, that all their labors would harmonize in the end, and the result would be a temple of beauty.   Now, God is our Great Architect; he has placed us in this life to perform our special and different tasks, and though we can see in them only incompleteness, yet God can see that if we will faithfully perform those tasks they will harmonize in the end, and the results will be of benefit to ourselves, of use to others, and glory to Him.

POWER OF MIND OVER BODY.

As we have previously devoted a chapter to " Mind and Matter," our reflections in this connection will principally be confined to the effect of mind upon that particular form of matter called the human body. Here it will be necessary to state our entire disbelief in what is usually styled an axiom in philosophy, namely, " that every effect must have its cause, and every cause must have its effect." Both as a matter of reason and consciousness we deny this. What, for instance, is volition ? It is force in energy directed to some particular end. Whence comes this force ? We answer it originates in the invisible mind. Mind is in itself a first cause so far as volition is concerned. And the same thing can not be observed of matter. The materialist assumes that mind is not distinct from matter, or that mind is not an entity separate and apart from matter. If this assumption was true, then it would make man a mere machine to be acted upon and moved by physical causes. If matter has properties peculiar to itself so has mind, and one of these properties is that it can originate causes. This is its nature ; it is one of its attributes of which all the ingenious reasoning of man cannot deprive it. Starting then from this stand-point, the explanation will become easy as to how mind can gain such mastery over the material body. It can animate and move it. It can fill it with health when wrongly directed with disease and suffering. When rightly directed by faith and knowledge it can purge the body from all pain and impurities.

Now, while this power has been seen and recognized in all ages and countries, even by the so-called learned physicians, yet they have always sought to limit this power or to share it with visible chemicals and drugs. A prominent London physician recently sent a communication to the *St. James Gazette*, from which we condense the following statement : " You say you 'do not quite grasp the scientific reasons' which I have tried to adduce for the assertion that if a sufferer from even ' incurable disease' will ' only firmly make up his mind that he is going to get well, in many cases his confidence will be justified.' These words were not precisely the words I used, but I will adopt them. The ' scientific reasons' are these : There is in ninety-nine cases out of a hundred, a possibility of finding a *modus vivendi* with disease, even though it be organic and ' incurable.' The very first condition of life is hope : ' While there is life there is hope,' and when hope dies life is no longer ' worth living.' Nature is not an artisan but an ar:ist, and with the aid of the 'ghost' (or spirit) she has contrived to put a good deal of 'artistic finish' into her chief work—man. This spirit is the life of the creation, and it is a life with more than one source, if I may so say. Many live by mental and nervous energy. The multitude of this last class of livers is very great; their bodies are wondrously weak and crippled, but their 'go' and 'spirit' are remarkable, and they live when those around them think they ought to die. Each case must be dealt with individually; but the task of finding a *modus vivendi* with 'incurable disease' is not difficult, and if one be found, the very fact of relieving the diseased organ from the task of playing first role in the drama of life will, in a majority of instances, help to check the malady by which it is affected.

"When a man hopes, his brain is stimulated, his nervous system is healthily excited, his vital energy is increased. Is it not obvious that if the vital energy be increased disease may be conquered, or at least outlived and downlived? Forgive me for being so prolix in trying to be plain."

Now, although the writer above quoted calls this exercise of mind power by the simple name of hope, we shall not wait here to dispute about terms. We take it to be an admission on his part that there is an invisible something that has an incalculable and wondrous power in curing disease, when the visible drug proves ineffec-

tual.   The homœopath says, that the allopath is a poi-
soner ; the allopath calls the homœopath a quack ;
while the eclectic claims to be wiser than both.   But
while they all admit the great power of mind as a curative agent they also claim that without the administration of drugs, according to their own learned method,
that diseases could not be cured.   But just at this point
the magnetic healer steps in, and he says, "away with
your drugs, throw physic to the dogs ; I can cure by
the invisible agent of magnetism, while you signally
and wofully fail by the application of your visible nostrums."   But permanent cures even by magnetism are
by no means so certain as its votaries are wont to claim
for it.   At one time there was a great rage for magnets,
but notwithstanding the numerous experiments on the
subject, no satisfactory conclusions have been arrived
at on the subject.   It is now about a century ago that
experiments of this nature were first made, and yet
to-day it is by no means established that the magnet is
of any remedial value whatever.   Professor Charcot, of
Paris, made many experiments on patients with magnets, and he states that he has no faith whatever in the
remedial efficacy of the magnet, except as it influenced
the imagination of the patient.   This is another admission of the power of mind, though Mons. Charcot tries
to limit and explain it by the word imagination.

History is replete with cases showing the effect of

mind over the body. There is the account of the man who was condemned to death for a crime that has been so frequently set forth in medical works. Some physicians obtained permission from the authorities to perform an experiment on this man previous to his execution. They bandaged his eyes, laid him on a couch, and caused him to hold his head over a bucket of water. They then punctured his neck with a small instrument, but not sufficient to cause the blood to flow. But they tried to convey to his mind the belief that the blood was flowing, by dropping some water from a smaller utensil into the bucket. At first they caused the water to drop slowly, and then increased its falling. As this increased the man grew faint, his face became livid, his pulse became weaker and weaker, and the experimenters believing the man would die, ceased their operations and he at once resumed his wonted vitality. But why, it may be asked, cite these cases from written history? Every-day observation will furnish us with proofs on the subject. The best authorities are almost unanimous in their belief that there is no sure cure for confirmed habits of inebriety unless the efforts in that direction are aided by a strong exercise of the will. In those localities that are subject to attacks of cholera or deadly fevers, all observers are agreed that more persons die through fear than from any other cause.

Another leading English physician, in writing to the
London Times in 1884, has some pertinent remarks
upon the effect that the mind has over the body. We
make the following extracts from his communication :

. "Now, the first observation I am anxious to make is,
that in the majority—yes, without hesitation, I affirm,
the majority—of these cases it is not true that the lives
of the condemned will be one year, or even one day,
shorter than the average longevity of persons of their
age and class who are presumed to be perfectly healthy.
I will go further and say this—the dread they endure
and the precautions they are compelled to take not
only do not tend to lengthen their lives, but are calculated to abridge them.   Long and careful observation
of what are called "diseased lives" has led me to the
conclusion that, eliminating the depressing and morbid
influence of that self-consciousness which is bred of a
condemned or suspected life, a man is just as well as he
feels, taking the average of a sufficient period to cover
the cycle of an average mode of existence.   Most lives,
however monotonous they may be, are marked by a
certain rhythmical succession "of ups and downs."
Take the mean of these and that will be the standard
and base of probabilities as regards the reasonable " ex-
pectancy" of life, let what will be the matter with the
individual.   Disease kills more victims through the
mind then by the body.   If medicine were so precise

a science that a "prognosis" could be worked out on
trustworthy data, something like authority might be
held to attach to the dictum of the family doctor or
consulting physician ; but this is not the fact, and observation and experience combine to show that the duration of any particular life is beyond ken and out of
reach of even shrewd guessing until the approach of
death is indicated by signs intelligible to all.

"What is the moral to be drawn from these general
conclusions ? Simply this—let no one, young or old,
be so foolish as to be depressed by the *dictum* of the
physician or surgeon who, with portentous shake of the
head, gives a despairing opinion. I repeat, that I
believe that more persons are killed by 'the fear of
death' than by disease.

" I know these assertions will be stigmatized as rash,
and I shall be condemned for making them ; but I do
so advisedly ; I believe medicine as a science discredits
medicine as an art. I am quite sure it does as far as
prognosis is concerned. On the other hand, medicine
as an art owes as much, or more, to the ministry of
hope as to the influence of drugs."

Surely these opinions, coming from a man who was
taught from his youth to believe that any disease would
succumb to drugs, if only the right ones could be
administered, are entitled to our serious consideration.
Who can be blamed, after such opinions as these, from
doubting the power of drugs to cure disease ?

LAWS OF NATURE.

In the presentation of the theory of the mind-cure to persons who have never given the subject any consideration, amongst the common objections made are the following : " But you do not profess to cure in opposition to the laws of nature ? Do you work in harmony with the laws of nature ? Do you not recognize that there are peculiarities in certain diseases ; and have not certain herbs and mineral substances qualities stamped upon them by their creator, and that, do what you will, you have to follow the laws and methods of nature or you must fail in your operations ?" To all these questions we answer, that we work in accordance with the laws of God, and not in opposition to them. The only difference between us is, that we call to our aid the laws of invisible mind, and not the laws that bind and govern material drugs. There are men calling themselves philosophers, who write very learnedly about the laws of nature—they use technical terms and reason after the most approved scholastic methods of logic—but though they turn their logic mills very artistically, yet they do not grind us out one kernel of nourishing corn. They

are like some of the equations in algebraic school books
—there are plus and minus, a great deal of study and
differentiating, but when the problem is finished we find
that it ends in zero.   After all the learned treatises that
have been written about the laws of nature, what do
we know of them, what can we say of them ?   The
only complete definition that we can give of the laws
of nature is, that they are the laws which produce the
phenomena of nature.   We cannot go behind them, and
we cannot explain the why and the wherefore of either
the laws or the phenomena.   Who can explain why one
seed put into the ground should produce a blue flower,
and another a red—a third an oak and another a pine
tree.   If we say these things produce after their kind, we
make no explanation of the fact—we merely affirm that
things are as they are.

We are accustomed to say that the laws of nature act
with unerring uniformity.   But what do we know of
their uniformity ?   That uniformity may be cut off or
abrogated by the intervention of some other law.   Let
a man stand in the middle of a room, holding in his
hand a small piece of steel—he opens his hand with the
palm downwards and the steel falls to the floor.   Why
does it fall?   In obedience to the law of gravitation,
one of the widest and best known of the laws of nature.
Suppose, instead of falling to the floor it had ascended
to the ceiling and there adhered ?   " But this is not pos-

sible," says some one, "for that would be contrary to a well-known law of nature." By no means. Place a magnet of sufficient force in the ceiling, and your steel flies upwards in obedience to the law of the magnet, and this law is just as much a law of nature, and no more and no less, as the law of gravitation. It is a law of nature that if water is subjected to a certain cold temperature that it will become solid ice, but that law will be rendered inoperative and overcome by the warm rays of the sun. They are both equally the laws of nature, though acting apparently in opposite directions. These examples will serve as illustrations of the fact that there is no such thing as constant uniformity in the operation of any law. Other laws are brought into play that render these laws inoperative. So that we can lay down no laws for nature and say that they are never contravened. All we can do, is to observe the operations, record them, and learn wisdom and humility.

Now, what do we know of the laws of mind? We answer, almost nothing. It is only here and there that we have observed a few facts, and from these we have not as yet been enabled to formulate but few principles. But what we do know is sufficient to convince us that the laws of mind can override the laws of matter and hold them as nothing. So that when we say a thing cannot be done because it is in opposition to the laws of nature, let us consider that until we

know all the laws of nature and all the laws of mind,
we are not in a position to pronounce anything impossible. Fortunately, we have facts both in sacred and
secular history that convince us of the almost omnipotent power of mind over matter and its laws. Christ
did not walk the water by destroying a law of nature,
but by calling to his aid the law of mind, and by the
aid of this law he performed his so-called miracles and
effected marvelous cures. And as in essence we are
sure that our minds are one with God, so in proportion
to our possession of the same, and faith in its power,
we ' shall be enabled to overcome all other laws and
effect cures. And, however learnedly people may talk
about the laws of nature, and what is impossible, we
have facts that set their opinions and prophecies at
defiance, for we hold that in the direction of our work
all things are possible with God.

DISEASE AND ITS REMEDIES.

What is disease ? It is the result of a departure from the spiritual laws of God. Its true cause is not to be attributed to the presence, absence, or decay of any part or parts of the human system. These disarrangements are the effects and not the causes of the disease. To remedy this state of things we have not to seek to build up materiality, but to aim at once to call to our aid the power of spirit. Our duty in this direction, we apprehend, is so plain that it needs no further words to make it clear. This being conceded, the question arises, with what agents should we approach these mental causes ? Matter, we have already seen, does not control or move mind. It is mind that controls and moves matter. Matter being non-intelligent, what effect can it have upon intelligent minds ? As this matter in itself has neither sense, feeling nor will, it can have no dynamic power over mind, and can make no departure from God's spiritual laws, so that we entirely put aside and ignore it as a curative agent. The very simplicity of this method should be sufficient to recommend it to the reflective mind. In mechanics,

other things being equal, the simplest machines are the
most efficient.   " It is surprising," says a philosopher,
"how all things in the universe resolve themselves into
results of a few principles at last."   In chemistry, many
things that were once considered to be primary elements
have been found to be compounds, so that at last the
chemist may find that his metals and minerals are but
the results of a very few primary elements.   In the
science of color, for instance—a few years ago a man
would have been styled a fanatic or a madman, who
would have denied the existence of seven primary
colors.   Those who were supposed to know most on
the subject proved beyond a doubt that it required
seven primary colors from which to make all other
colors and shades of color, namely: violet, indigo, blue,
green, yellow, orange and red.   But how stands the
fact to-day ?   They now only recognize three primaries,
namely : blue, yellow and red.   Some German philosopher asserts that the time will come when all colors
will be shown to be composed of two original colors.
This cannot be scoffed at as a mere freak of the imagination, for it must be recollected that most of the different
chemical substances are not different because they are
composed of different ingredients, but because of their
different proportions of the same elements.   Starch,
sugar, vinegar and alcohol, are very dissimilar in their
nature and effects, but they are all alike composed of

the same elements. It is only the different proportions in which these elements are mixed together that give them their distinctive differences. Now, the names of disease is legion, but we trace them to one cause, and for them we have but one cure.

The world has for ages been perplexed, mystified and imposed upon by the so-called science of medicine. A list of technical and high-sounding words and phrases have been wrapped around diseases and their remedies until the multitude stands in awe of the long array. It is too often the case that people reverence what they do not understand. Call whiskey by its medical name, *"spiritus frumenti,"* and it at once inspires respect. Instead of saying that a child has measles, state that it is afflicted with *"rubiola,"* and the same disease with different names is thought to be two distinct diseases. Now, we desire to tear aside this word-fringe, and let in the light of Divine truth upon the whole mass of jargon and quackery.

Even amongst physicians we find skeptics regarding the utility of their own practice. Many openly admit that they have no very confident faith in the certainty of their art, and some deny the possibility of their ever constructing a scientific system of remedial methods. " Medicine," says Papillon, " may be summed up as the application of certain sciences. Whenever these sciences may advance, that art should do so also." But whatever may be said of the other sciences, we deny that the science of medicine, as a curative or preventive system, has advanced one step—and this is because the agents it employs are false. Medical men have given their time, talents and learning, to the subject ; but in spite of them, diseases have increased and multiplied. Their studies with regard to the human system—its construction, functions of the organs, their diseases and treatment—are divided as follows: Anatomy teaches how the organs are made ; physiology how they perform their functions in a healthy state; pathology how they discharge them in a diseased state ; and therapeutics how they discharge them in regard to media, that is to say, the medial agencies of every kind with which they may be brought in contact. Now, the modern physician relies upon all these for his knowledge how to ward off or cure disease. With the first two, anatomy and physiology, we have no quarrel, but against pathology and therapeutics we proclaim a bold and open war. The practice of medical men, in these directions, has been fraught with incalculable mischief to the health of the community. The most honest and outspoken of them have so confessed.

Dr. Benjamin Rush has said: " It is impossible to calculate the mischief Hippocrates has done by first marking nature with his name, and afterwards letting her loose upon sick people."

Dr. Mason Good, a learned professor in London, said : " the effects of medicine on the human system are in the highest degree uncertain, except, indeed, that they have already destroyed more lives than war, pestilence and famine combined."

Dr. Benjamin Waterhouse, professor in Harvard University, says : " I am sick of learned quackery."

Some other distinguished physician has said : " It would be better for mankind if all the drugs were thrown into the sea, but worse for the fishes."

Dr. James Johnson, of England, surgeon-extraordinary to the king, says : "I declare my conscientious opinion, founded on long observation and reflection, that if there was not a single physician, surgeon, apothecary, man-midwife, chemist, druggist or drug on the face of the earth, there would be less sickness and less mortality."

Why these failures ? Mainly because the physician of to-day has followed in the footsteps of his predecessors. He reads in his books that certain diseases are known by certain symptoms, and that certain drugs administered according to the quantity and method laid down, will effect cures. His diagnosis is often of the shallowest kind, but even when correct his remedies are still of the conventional description, and if, through the vitality of the patient or by the power of mind, a cure is effected, he tries to convince his patient that his recovery is entirely due to his careful administration of the prescribed drugs. Thus a false over-arching faith has grown up in the efficacy of these poisons. The Israelites of old are no more to be condemned for their worship of the golden calf set up in the wilderness, than are the masses for their idolatry of the medical drugs set up amidst humanity in these days of enlightenment. We are endeavoring to wean them from their false faith, and point them to the only true God. The magicians have thrown down their rods, and now we throw down our rod of mind-cure, and it will swallow up all the rest.

SCRIPTURAL ARGUMENTS.

We have as yet taken no position for which we cannot find scriptural authority. The good Bishop Cumberland said : " I read my Bible as I read a book of facts, and I put upon those facts such an interpretation as an enlightened Christian conscience enables me to do." This is just the liberty we take for ourselves and concede to others. We are advancing no new doctrine, but only aiming to give force and vitality to an old one —a doctrine taught and practised by the Master. It appears to be assumed by large masses of church members, that Christianity consists in passing a life of praise and prayer, and preaching against the moral evils of the world. Christ taught both by precept and example that one of the chief duties of life was to cure suffering and banish bodily disease. The ancient temples were at once church and hospital. The early Christians were healers, conceiving it to be their imperative duty to follow in Christ's footsteps, for they felt the truth of the saying, " Except ye have the spirit of Christ ye are none of his." We feel that it is one of the most damaging omissions in the lives of modern Christians that sufficient prominence has not been given to the healing of disease. And, further, though they speak of faith as a necessary thing to spiritual salvation, yet they have lost sight of it as a word full of meaning, and having direct reference to the curing of all bodily disease. Christ constantly spoke of faith as the great and grand requisite in everything, especially to the curing of disease. He never advised his followers to have recourse to the use of drugs, for he did not use them himself, evidently not recognizing them as useful or necessary agents. Let us follow him through some of his journeys, and aim to learn lessons therefrom. We subjoin several passages from the scriptures, with their places of reference. When he had ended his sermon on the mount, wherein he spake as man never spake, the first act he performed was to cure a case of bodily infirmity:

"When he was come down from the mountain, great multitudes followed him. And behold, there came a leper and worshipped him, saying, Lord, if thou wilt, thou canst make me clean. And Jesus put forth his hand, and touched him, saying, I will, be thou clean. And immediately his leprosy was cleansed." Matt. 8; 1, 2, 3.

Here we take occasion to remark that this was an exhibition of the omnipotence of mind over matter. We desire to record not only cases of cure, but also to state events wherein he showed the power of mind over inanimate things.

" And when he was entered into a ship, his disciples followed him. And behold, there arose a great tempest in the sea, insomuch that the ship was covered with the waves, but he was asleep. And his disciples came to him and awoke him, saying, Lord, save us ; we perish. And he saith unto them, Why are ye fearful, O ye of little faith ! Then he arose, and rebuked the winds and the sea ; and there was a great calm." Matt. 8 ; 23 to 26.

"And behold, they brought to him a man sick of the palsy, lying on a bed ; and Jesus, seeing their faith, said unto the sick of the palsy, Son, be of good cheer ; thy sins are forgiven thee." Matt. 10 ; 2.

In the above quotation it will be observed that sickness is spoken of as a sin. It will be necessary to bear this in mind, for it is by sin that diseases are in the world, and in proportion as we overcome sin we destroy disease ; but we can never overcome sin by the use of drugs.

Again, in Matt. 9 ; 1 to 29, it is recorded :

"While he spake these things unto them, behold, there came a certain ruler, and worshiped him, saying, My daughter is even now dead : but come and lay thy hand upon her and she shall live. And Jesus arose, and followed him, and *so did* his disciples. (And behold, a woman which was diseased with an issue of blood twelve years, came behind him, and touched the hem of his garment.   For she said within herself, If I may but touch his garment, I shall be whole.   But Jesus turned him about, and when he saw her, he said, Daughter, be of good comfort: thy faith hath made thee whole.   And the woman was made whole from that hour.)   And when Jesus came into the ruler's house, and saw the minstrels and the people making a noise, he said unto them, Give place : for the maid is not dead, but sleepeth.   And they laughed him to scorn. But when the people were put forth, he went in, and took her by the hand, and the maid arose.   And the fame hereof went abroad into all that land.   And when Jesus departed thence, two blind men followed him, crying, and saying, Thou son of David, have mercy on us.   And when he was come into the house, the blind men came to him: and Jesus saith unto them, Believe ye that I am able to do this?   They said unto him, Yea, Lord.   Then touched he their eyes, saying, According to your faith, be it unto you."

The great lesson in the above to be learned is, that the power of faith in those possessing disease is sometimes a necessary element.

As the parable of the sower has some bearing upon the thorough success in some cases of the faith or mind-cure, we here quote it : "And he spake many things unto them in parables, saying, Behold, a sower went forth to sow ; and when he sowed some seeds fell by the way-side, and the fowls came and devoured them up ; some fell upon stony places, where they had not much earth ; and forthwith they sprung up, because they had no deepness of earth : and when the sun was up, they were scorched ; and because they had no root, they withered away. And some fell among thorns ; and the thorns sprung up, and choked them : but other fell into good ground, and brought forth fruit, some an hundred-fold, some sixty-fold, some thirty-fold. Who hath ears to hear, let him hear."—Matt. 13; 7 to 9.

Indeed, so necessary does faith seem to be in the case of some persons, that it appears to be almost impossible to cure them without their own individual faith in the power of God to restore them to health. Hence, it is recorded of Christ's sojourn in a certain place : " And he did not many mighty works there, because of their unbelief."

Below will be found several scriptural accounts of cases of cure : "And when they were come to the multitude, there came to him a certain man kneeling down to him, and saying, Lord, have mercy on my son ; for he is a lunatic, and sore vexed, for oft-times he falleth into the fire, and oft into the water. And I brought him to thy disciples, and they could not cure him. Then Jesus answered and said, O faithless and perverse generation, how long shall I be with you? How long shall I suffer you ? Bring him hither to me. And Jesus rebuked the devil, and he departed out of him : and the child was cured from that very hour. Then came the disciples to Jesus apart, and said, Why could not we cast him out ? And Jesus said unto them, Because of your unbelief : for verily I say unto you, If ye have faith as a grain of mustard-seed, ye shall say unto this mountain, Remove hence to yonder place, and it shall remove ; and nothing shall be impossible unto you."— Matt. 16 ; 14 to 20.

" And behold, two blind men sitting by the wayside, when they heard that Jesus passed by, cried out, saying, Have mercy on us, O Lord, thou son of David. And the multitude rebuked them, because they should hold their peace ; but they cried the more, saying, Have mercy on us, O Lord, thou son of David. And Jesus stood still, and called them, and said, What will ye that I shall do unto yon? They say unto him, Lord, that our eyes may be opened. So Jesus had compassion on them, and touched their eyes : and immediately their eyes received sight, and they followed him."—Matt. 20; 30 to 34.

" And behold, there was a woman which had a spirit of infirmity eighteen years, and was bowed together, and could in no wise lift up herself. And when Jesus saw her, he called her to him, and said unto her, Woman, thou art loosed from thine infirmity. And he laid his hands on her ; and immediately she was made straight, and glorified God."—Luke 14; 11 to 13.

"And as he entered into a certain village, there met him ten men that were lepers, which stood afar off, and they lifted up their voices, and said, Jesus, Master, have mercy on us. And when he saw them, he said unto them, Go shew yourselves unto the priests. And it came to pass, that, as they went, they were cleansed."— Luke 17; 12 to 14.

"Then when Mary was come where Jesus was, and saw him, she fell down at his feet, saying unto him, Lord, if thou hadst been here, my brother had not died. When Jesus therefore saw her weeping, and the Jews also weeping which came with her, he groaned in the spirit, and was troubled, and said, Where have ye laid him? They say unto him, Lord, come and see. Jesus wept. Then said the Jews, Behold how he loved him! And some of them said, Could not this man, which opened the eyes of the blind, have caused that even this man should not have died? Jesus therefore again groaning in himself, cometh to the grave. It was a cave, and a stone lay upon it. Jesus said, Take ye away the stone. Martha, the sister of him that was dead, saith unto him, Lord, by this time he stinketh: for he hath been dead four days. Jesus saith unto her, Said I not unto thee, that if thou wouldst believe, thou shouldst see the glory of God? Then they took away

the stone from the place where the dead was laid.   And
Jesus lifted up his eyes, and said, Father, I thank thee
that thou hast heard me : And I knew that thou hear-
est me always ; but because of the people which stand
by, I said it, that they may believe that thou hast sent
me.   And when he had thus spoken, he cried with a
loud voice, Lazarus, come forth.   And he that was dead
came forth, bound hand and foot with grave-clothes ;
and his face was bound about with a napkin.   Jesus
saith unto them, Loose him, and let him go."—St. John,
11 ; 32 to 44.

The above are some of the instances of cure by
Christ.   It might be here objected that though Christ
effected these cures, yet that they were done by a miraculous power.   Now, we do not believe in miracles,
that is, as the popular mind understands them.   Many
persons' ideas of miracles are that they are effects
brought about by the rescinding, cutting off or over-
riding the laws of nature, which, after all, are the laws
of God.   But we say that God's laws never have been
and never can be set aside or contravened.   Those
things recorded in the New Testament as miracles, and
the thousands of things that have occurred since the
days of Christ that are looked upon as miracles, are no
miracles at all.   They are the results of laws that are
brought into play, of which the mass of people are ignorant.   Christ never claimed to perform miracles.

What he did was entirely in accordance with the laws of God. He did not even claim that he alone possessed the power to perform the things which he did ; on the other hand, he said to his followers, "The works that I do ye shall do, and greater than these." Peter cured the lame man, Paul restored the cripple, and Christ's disciples everywhere went about curing diseases. When they brought to him cases which he could not cure, he simply said to them, "O ye of little faith."

In closing this chapter it will be pertinent to refer to a very common expression that falls from the lips of even good Christians. When sickness overtakes them they speak of it as an affliction from God. In one sense this is right, and from another view it is entirely wrong. Sickness is an affliction from God because it is the result of a violation of God's laws. In Lamentations iii, 33: "For he doth not afflict willingly, nor grieve the children of men." David says: "No good thing will he withhold from them who walketh uprightly." He is able and willing to cure all sickness and sorrow in those who will seek him aright. In Ex. xxiii, 25 : He promises that if the people will hearken unto his voice, He will take sickness away from the midst of them. In ii Chronicle, 16 : 12, it is written: "And Asa in the thirty and ninth year of his reign was diseased in his feet, until his disease *was* exceeding *great :* yet in his disease he sought not to the LORD, but to the physicians.   And Asa slept with his fathers."

Since the days of Asa, just how many have slept with their fathers because they "sought not to the Lord but to the physicians," it is impossible to tell.   Doubtless many millions.   As many more have lived lives of suffering because their whole system has been poisoned with drugs.

DECLARATION OF PRINCIPLES.

While in San Francisco, California, engaged in effecting cures and teaching the science of metaphysical healing, in the summer of 1884, the *Evening Bulletin*, a paper that for respectability and thought was considered to occupy a leading position among the journals of that coast, made some strictures on the healing method. We were invited to make a brief statement of our views and claims, for publication in that paper. This we did, and as readers like to see both sides of the question discussed, we print the communication and the editor's answer, both appearing in the same issue :

FAITH CURE AND MIND CURE.

EDITOR BULLETIN :—In your last Friday's issue appeared an article under the above heading, which though it contained some truths, yet gave but an imperfect outline of the position and claims of this new science. As I have had considerable practice both as a healer and teacher in metaphysical science, or as it is popularly called "the mind cure," I venture to ask for space in your journal to set forth what we believe, and also what we claim to be able to perform.

First—We contend that disease, whatever form it may assume, is mental and not physical ; in other words, that all diseases are but effects, having their origin in the regions of mind and not of matter. This will seem to persons of the old school, a radical position to take, and yet a careful observation of the writings of all practitioners reveal the fact that they have always recognized while administering their drugs, that after all, the cheerfulness, the hope, the faith, or to put it tersely, the mind of the patients, is the great factor in restoring them to health. What is this but admitting that despondency, dread, apprehension and fear are the great products of disease ?

Second—we ignore drugs in whatever form administered, as perfectly worthless curative agents. All outward agents of whatever nature, although they may for a time appear to cure disease, yet, in the end, prove worthless. They are delusions and snares. They for a time cover up diseases, which reappear in their first or some other form. While many persons are compelled by facts to admit that cures have been effected by our method, they say that the diseases so cured are always what medical men call of a nervous kind. This is not true. We recognize no limit, and acknowledge no classification.

Third—We believe in one eternal and unchangeable God, who is the same to-day, yesterday and for ever.

From Him cometh every good and perfect gift—even the gift of healing of disease. The early Christians always practiced the gifts of healing—and declared that those gifts came from God. Christians of to-day, of whatever sect, will not dare to deny that Christ and his followers possessed and practiced the power of healing, but they seem disposed to doubt whether these powers have descended to modern times. We answer these doubts by an appeal to facts to be found in San Francisco and elsewhere. We recognize no permanent curative agent except the universal mind or God. The better we live, the closer becomes our relation to God, and we can draw from this universal fountain the power, which if applied by knowledge, is equal to the curing of "all the ills which flesh is heir to." We hear much in these days of the power of magnetism, and the influence which departed spirits have upon the human organism. Whatever powers these may have, we know that they are of a limited and even doubtful character. All human beings are spirits and as such can hold communion with the Infinite Spirit, and need not depend upon departed friends to do the work in this mundane sphere which they can do themselves.

Fourth—As all persons can work out problems in mathematics when they understand the principles, so any one can produce harmony in music by ruling out the discord. So also can any one bring health and harmony into their lives when they understand God's laws, and how to apply them.   Disease is a discord, an error, and we recognize no power beneath the Divine to remove it.   When this is recognized and acted upon, the problem of disease or discord in God's children will be solved, and harmony, health and happiness will reign upon the earth.

In penning this I am conscious that I may expose myself to the ridicule of some, and to the skepticism of others.   These things have always been the heritage of those who have dared to step aside from the beaten track, but Divine power and the world of fact will in the end win them over.   We feel with the old thinkers " that one, with God, is a majority."   God layeth his hand on slowly, but His power is irresistible.   I regret that I cannot more fully express myself, but as my space must necessarily be limited in a journal that is published in so many public interests, I subscribe myself, respectfully,   JULIA ANDERSON ROOT.

The learned editor replied as follows :

THE GIFT OF HEALING.

"An editorial which appeared in this paper some days ago on faith and mind cures has elicited a reply, which appears in another column.   Of course the writer does not agree with the views expressed in this journal.   It is presumed that there is such a thing as the philosophy

of disease, including, of course, remedial agents. But
the diagnosis which our correspondent gives is not con-
sistent with any philosophy which has thus far been
recognized in the world. It is simply that all diseases
originate in the mind. They are mere discords of the
soul, to be cured by a direct interposition of Providence,
which amounts to a miraculous intervention applied to
personal healing. This theory discards all secondary
agents, such as drugs and the help of skilled physicians
who know minutely the whole human anatomy, and who
have had the advantage of the best medical training
which the world affords. It relegates the healing art
to a class of persons who ignore the physical system
both from policy and because they actually know nothing about it, and who prefer, for their own conscience,
to locate all diseases of the mind, and to call for divine
assistance in removing them, counting human skill as
nothing.

Now, there is a class of diseases which possibly can
be treated in this way with some benefit to the patient.
In some cases the disease is nothing more than a delusion. There is a theory that the majority of the people are not sane on all subjects. There is some degree
of abnormalism. That, however, is a fanciful theory,
founded on nothing more than a class of mental phenomena which have a close connection with bodily in-
firmities. To say that the victim of neuralgia or dys-

pepsia, or of a consuming fever, or of the small-pox, has no physical disease, that his ailments are simply the result of a disease in his mind, or a disease which is to be located there, is simply absurd. The skeptic has a good right to call at once for a demonstration. The individual whose mind is in a perfectly healthy condition is prostrated with a fever or some actual disease, of course his mind, as a consequence, is affected by his bodily condition. But that is a secondary consideration. The mind cure in all this class of cases is perfectly hopeless. The disease is not there. It is not a discord in the mind of the patient, but it is a poison in his physical system. That cannot be removed by laying on of hands, nor by any degree of faith in an unseen power. There never has been a well authenticated case in modern times where a patient was cured in the last stages of consumption by any medication of his mind, such as is involved in the faith-cure theory— not a single instance where a malignant cancer has been cured by faith, or a crushed limb restored.

Now, there is a class of diseases, partly fictitious and partly real, which are limited to the nervous system and the mind of the victim. If the individual is under a delusion that something ails him, that is the disease. No doubt there are thousands in this condition. The world is full of delusions. What is needful in such cases is to remove the delusion, and if it can be removed by another delusion, perhaps the end justifies the means. It might better accord with the truth to tell the patient that nothing ails him. But in a morbid condition of mind that will not always do. Old Dr. Abernethy and other God-fearing physicians would have told such patients that nothing under the heavens ailed them, and that their chief need was to get out into the bracing atmosphere, and take more cheerful views of life.

Just here is room for the play of all sorts of quackery. How many cures have been effected by administering bread pills? That was an old application of the faith cure. The patient believed that there was great virtue in the medicine and so got well—that is, escaped from his delusion. In every insane asylum the skillful physician knows that a majority of his patients are suffering from delusions which are brought on by a bad condition of the physical system. He knows just how far he can go with his mind cure; but he knows well enough that he cannot reach that ultimatum without first searching for disease in the physical system and applying his remedies there.

On the theory which our correspondent promulgates, what a beneficent work might be wrought in these asylums by the faith-cure practice ! There are a thousand people in a single institution, all under some sort of a delusion. Once remove this and the patient is well.

It is only a discord in the mind ! No doubt, any form of mental delusion is in the direction of insanity. It is a symptom of unsound mentality. If the symptoms progress far enough a case of insanity is recorded. But in a majority of such cases some well-chosen remedial agent, such as a change of climate, travel, medicine wisely administered, is all that is needful for the complaining party. And sometimes to be told bluntly that there is no serious thing the matter, is a potent remedy.

The province of faith cure and mind cure we conceive to be to exorcise from the mind of the patient his delusions. The taint of mental abnormalism is now so wide-spread that there is room for remedies included in faith cure and mind cure. These remedies cannot be applied to physical ills in any other than an indirect way. When it is perceived that the mind is acting unfavorably upon the body, a restoration of the one will have a beneficial influence on the other. This class of nervous diseases come in time to affect the body, producing insomnia, low spirits, loss of tone and vitality. Of course if the mind can be brought into a healthy condition, the result will go a long way toward restoring a healthy tone to the physical system. But when one is run over by a locomotive and his legs are mashed to a jelly, the faith cure must be counted out. If anything saves him it will be the surgeon's knife and good nursing. When a victim is overtaken by the yellow fever and the poison is all in his veins, or the cholera which collapses his stomach, the trouble is not primarily in his mind. It is absurd to refer this disease to any such source, and it would be arrant quackery to depend upon the expedients recognized as belonging to the faith or mind cure. In the latter class of remedies there is room for the occult and the mysterious. To this day great dependence is placed upon the incantations and pow-wow of medicine men among uncivilized and half-civilized people. But among enlightened people it is supposed that such remedies are discarded; or they only furnish fresh illustrations of the delusions which have not yet been banished from the world."

In the above criticism the editor appears to have made some points against this science, without really having done so. When we say that disease originates in the mind, we do not mean in all cases that it originates in the mind of the patient or particular person suffering from disease, but that it has its origin at some time or other in the error, mistake or discord of mortal mind. Man is mysteriously connected mentally with his fellows. It was Pythagoras who said that if there is one poor suffering soul in this universe, all other souls will be affected until that suffering soul is restored to health. The error, the discord of one is the error and discord of the whole, liable to be acted upon by fear and other agents, and made manifest as circumstances may dictate. The editor is further in error when he says that neuralgia, dyspepsia, or consuming fever cannot be cured by this method. We recognize no limit to this power when properly applied. Of course we do not ignore the necessity of conditions. Christ himself recognized the necessity of conditions in effecting cures. What does it mean when it is stated : "And He could do no mighty works there because of their unbelief"? Here was an admission that belief or faith was a necessary element to success in those particular cases. If a man should come to us with a disease, and obstinately refuse to believe that we could cure him, or strongly doubted that we had any power whatever to do him any good, these fears and doubts would go a long way in keeping him in his diseased condition. But with the perfect knowledge in the mind of the operator, and a perfect faith in the mind of the patient, we recognize no limit to the cure of any class of disease. For the truth of this we appeal to facts, some of which are to be found elsewhere in this work. We do not desire to follow the learned editor through all his objections and quasi-objections. What he urges mainly against the mind-cure can be urged against cures by any method or process whatever.

HEREDITY AND LONGEVITY.

We need no statistics to prove to us the fearful prevalence of disease and suffering. In one shape or other they are to be found in every locality and in almost every house. We may justly assume that a vast deal of suffering might be prevented by the use of judicious means within the reach of every individual. It is certain that the diseases and appetites of parents are transmitted to their offspring. We constantly find the children of those whe are addicted to the use of alcohol and tobacco, manifesting the same desire for these things as their progenitors. Though the habits, mind and disposition of the father have considerable influence in determining the physical, mental and moral condition of his offspring, yet they cannot be compared to the influences of the mother for good or for evil upon her children. These remarks are forcibly true of the period preceding the time when she becomes a mother. At these times mothers are in the habit of using vile drugs, and when this is not the case they often permit themselves to become violent in temper, or they indulge in desponding moods. These can be all obviated by a knowledge and application of metaphysical science. When mothers understand and act upon this great Truth, a speedy improvement will take place in the human race. Man is an animal, and more than an animal, and it is a shame to our civilization that the horse, the ox, the sheep and the hog have more cares bestowed on them in improving and perpetuating their species than man.

Montaigne, in his essay on the "Resemblance of "Children to their Fathers," says "there is a certain sort "of crafty humility that springs from presumption; as this, for example, that we confess our ignorance in many things, and are so courteous as to acknowledge that there are in works of nature some qualities and conditions that are imperceptible to us, and of which our understanding cannot discern the means and causes; by which honest declaration we hope to obtain that people shall also believe us of those that we say we do understand. We need not trouble ourselves to seek out miracles and strange difficulties; methinks there are such incomprehensible wonders amongst the things that we ordinarily see as surpass all difficulties of miracles." In his essay he goes on and applies these remarks to inherited peculiarities of character, figure, constitution and habits. Many things in nature can be referred to law, and we can readily prophecy with a degree of certainty as to what will occur, and sometimes tell the "how" of their occurrence. But in the matter of heredity this is not possible. However, the lesson is forced upon us that traits are inherited, and in some cases make their appearance after the lapse of two or three generations. Sometimes they pertain to the configuration of the body ; at other times to a peculiarity of the countenance ; while in many instances it is matters of disposition alone that are conspicuous. One or two of these may be mentioned. Montaigne states that in the family of Lepidus, at Rome, there were three, not successively, but by intervals, that were born with the same eye, covered with a cartilage. In Greece there was a family, almost every member of which had the crown of the head pointed like a lance-head ; all whose heads were not so formed being regarded as illegitimate. Some years ago there was on exhibition in Europe a father and son, named Jeftichjew, whose faces were so covered with hair as to give them the appearance of Skye terriers ; the hair was as soft and as white as the fur of the Angora cat. A well authenticated case is that of a family in England, named Lambert. The peculiarity affecting this family appeared first in the person of Edward Lambert, whose whole body, except the face, the palms of the hands, and the soles of the feet, was covered with a sort of shell, consisting of horny excrescences. He was the father of six children, all of whom, as soon as they had

reached the age of six weeks, presented the same peculiarity.   Only one of them lived ; he married and transmitted the peculiarity to all his sons.   For five generations all the male members of the family were distinguished by the horny excrescences which had adorned
the body of Edward Lambert.

There are many other cases of inherited physical
peculiarities which could be given, but the above instances will be found sufficient for the purposes of this
work.

The hereditary transmission of qualities will be generally admitted, whether they are physical, mental or
moral, and although wise and learned fathers do not
always possess wise and learned children, still there
can be no doubt of the transmission of intellectual
forces and tendencies.   If the ancestry of our poets,
historians, scientists and warriors could be traced, we
should find enough to convince us that they possessed
special powers, sufficient to account for the transcen-
dant powers in their offspring.

In this connection it will be well for our temperance
friends to learn a lesson, which to some extent will af ·
ford them argument against the use of stimulating
drinks by parents.   Dr. Howe says : " The children
of drunkards are deficient in bodily and vital energy,
and are predisposed by their very organization to have
a craving for alcoholic stimulants.   If they pursue the

course of their fathers, which they have more temptation to follow and less power to avoid than the children of the temperate, they add to their hereditary weakness, and increase the tendency to idiotcy or insanity in their constitution, and this they leave to their children after them."

A sermon was preached by Robert Collyer, of Chicago, entitled "The Thorn in the Flesh," from which we make the following extract: "In the far-reaching influences that go to every life, and away backward as certainly as forward, children are sometimes born with appetites fatally strong in their nature. As they grow up the appetite grows with them, and speedily becomes a master, the master or tyrant, and by the time he arrives at manhood the man is a slave. I heard a man say that for eight-and-twenty years the soul within him had to stand like an unsleeping sentinel, guarding his appetite for strong drink. To be a man at last, under such a disadvantage, not to mention a saint, is as fine a piece of grace as can well be seen. There is no doctrine that demands a larger vision than this of the depravity of human nature." Let the reader just think of this. A man for twenty-eight years beset by a demon, and yet not fall! Has the preacher overdrawn his picture? We do not want to discuss that total depravity doctrine, but we affirm that there was no necessity for that long besetment of temptation. Metaphys-

ical science says, " Resist the devil and he will flee
from you." Yea, the devil of appetite for strong drink.
We have known of cases cured, and we further affirm
that no outward circumstances without internal cure
will prove effective. So that in the temperance reform
metaphysical science is bound to play an important
part.

The question has often been discussed as to the
length of the term, if any, that Divine Providence has
affixed to the duration of human life. The expression
(Gen., 6–5) " His days shall be an hundred and twenty
years," has been estimated by some to mean that this
should be the extreme duration of life; others have
thought that it meant the average. It is certain that
the duration of life varies in different ages. Abraham
lived one hundred and five years. Joshua died at one
hundred and ten. When David wrote his Psalms,
eighty years was considered an extraordinary age. In
the 90th Psalm, verse 10, it is recorded : " The days
of our years are three-score years and ten ; and if by
reason of strength they be four-score years, yet is there
strength, labor and sorrow." However, there are many
cases in our times where persons have attained to a
greater age than this, and have passed their aged days
in comfort and peace. How long man, under the most
favorable circumstances, was intended to live, is a matter partly of observation and partly of conjecture. A

distinguished French scientist, P. Flourens, says : "The normal duration of human life may be treated in two ways, as Haller and Buffon have done—historically or physiologically. They sought historically what the natural, ordinary, and normal term of the life of man is, and they placed it between ninety and a hundred years. They afterwards sought, still historically, to learn what is the extreme limit of human life, and Haller has placed it at a little less than two centuries. Buffon thought that the total duration of life could be estimated by the period of growth." Now, if we take the limit of the complete growth in man and the following named animals to be as follows, we may be able to make some intelligent approximation as to the natural duration of life.

This completion takes place—

			DURATION OF LIFE.
In the	camel at 8 years.		About 40 years.
" "	horse	" 5 "	25 "
" "	ox	" 4 "	20 "
" "	dog	" 3 "	10 to 12 "
" "	cat	" 18 months.	9 to 10 "

Man is considered to be about twenty years in growing. If from the above table we conclude that animals live five times as long as their period of growth, then may we not conclude that man will live five times his period of growth, which would make the duration of human life one hundred years. But whether this is so or not, is not so much a matter of importance as the manner in which human beings lead their lives. A long life is not so much to be desired as a life of usefulness. Burke says: "Old age, when it has been attained in the paths of wisdom and virtue, claims universal honor and respect." An old age of that kind is to be desired, but there are cases where persons have lived long whose career has been one continued course of selfishness. Others have had their declining years marred and made miserable by diseases and pains which might have been prevented. Give us health, usefulness and long life. The metaphysical healer will bestow his time and talent not alone in curing diseases, but in preventing them he will prevent the impairment of health and the disturbing of the affections and intellect. He will, also, as opportunity may occur, instil into the minds of those with whom he comes in contact such ideas as will improve them spiritually, and thus lead them nearer to God. Wealth is a good thing to have, but too many sacrifice their lives and every noble feeling of manhood to obtain it. Their cry has been gold! gold!

> "Bright and yellow, hard and cold;
> Molten, graven, hammered and rolled;
> Heavy to get and light to hold;
> Hoarded, bartered, bought and sold;
> Stolen, borrowed, squandered, doled;
> Spurned by the young, but hugged by the old;
> To the very verge of the churchyard mould."

We must not lose sight of the fact that when we speak of longevity and its diseases, that mental and moral diseases are often as dangerous, and sometimes more so, than the so-called physical diseases. In no way is this more strikingly exhibited than in the insane craving for money, which some aged persons display up to the edge of the grave. The habit of grasping and hoarding has become so strong upon them, that they appear powerless to resist it. Of such souls we should say that they have wandered far from their Maker, and have missed the true object and aims of life. They neither love their fellow men nor their God. They are blind, torpid, and are neither friends, lovers nor citizens of the world, and can have no sympathy with mankind. They know nothing of human nor divine love. How admonishing in this connection are the words of Henry More :

> "But souls that of his own good life partake,
> He loves as his own self ; dear as his eye
> They are to Him ; He'll never them forsake :
> When they shall die, then God Himself shall die :
> They live, they live in blest eternity."

Metaphysical science says, desire to live long, but also desire to live well. Good actions are of more importance than longevity, but if we live in accordance with God's laws, both are attainable.

INSTRUCTIONS FOR HEALING.

All that we have advanced in previous chapters has either a direct or indirect bearing upon the subject of the present chapter, and it is absolutely necessary that the positions we have taken should be thoroughly understood, otherwise the student is not likely to meet with success in curing disease, either in himself or others. The conviction must be thoroughly implanted in the mind, that mind and matter are two distinct things, whether matter is in an organized or unorganized state. Next, that it is mind only that can feel, think and act, and the only thing in creation that possesses force.

For the truth of this proposition we do not rely simply upon mathematical demonstration and visible facts, but also upon that which is equally convincing, namely, innate consciousness. When a person says, " I " have a headache ; " I" have pain in the stomach; what is the " I"? Plainly, it is not the head nor the stomach that speaks. It is something outside and independent of these organs, for it speaks of them as being distinct from itself. Again, this " I " says, "My" head aches, " My " stomach pains "me," " My " hands

are cold, " My" feet are warm.   Here the " I " speaks
of " my" things—that is, that the "I " is not these organs, but that it owns them.   They are not me, but
mine—that is, I am something independent of them.
This something is the soul.

The position we take is, that the body and its organs
are but the correspondences of a spiritual body and
organs.   These spiritual organs are the real and lasting, while the material are but manifestations, and are
not lasting.   These material manifestations cannot control the spiritual, but the spiritual can and does control
the material.   Upon a true understanding and conviction of this great truth lies our success in healing.
Without this is understood, the student must turn back
to the contents of this book, and become thoroughly
imbued with the doctrines and truths herein taught.

Then, as we speak of the organs of the body as being
distinct from the soul, so we do of disease, and we address it as such.   If the healer has a critical or acute
case to treat, the patient should be addressed inaudibly
as follows : " You are distinct from your body and its
organs.   You have nothing to fear.   There is no danger.   ' You' are not sick ; ' you' are deceived."   Then
the healer should endeavor to find out the cause of the
sickness, so that he can address the disease by name,
and say to it, " You have no power to afflict this soul,
for it is immortal and one with God, and governed by

His unerring and unchanging law of love and harmony, and there is no discord in His government." Then, to prove that the patient is suffering only in belief, say that there is no life or intelligence in matter, and that the soul does not dwell in matter, but only acts upon it and has perfect control over it, and has it in its own power to say whether the matter shall suffer or not. Remember, it is mind acting upon matter, and not matter upon mind. This proves beyond a doubt that in a true sense there is really no illness. For as matter can feel only as the mind says it can, and the soul being perfect and not dwelling in matter, does not suffer. Then, what is it that suffers? It is the mortal mind, and over this the soul has supreme control when you choose to exercise it. The soul itself cannot be sick or subject to discord or error in any way or under any circumstances, for it is born of God and subject to His law only, and if the patient is not suffering from a sin against God's laws, he will speedily recover.

In treating a case of indigestion, which is one of the most prevalent diseases, say to the patient mentally: "Your stomach is not affected, it is in a perfectly healthy condition, and so are all the other organs; the blood is pure and circulates perfectly, and there is no inherited taint in the blood." If the case is consumption, dispute the evidence that there is any decay going on in the tissues. Learn, if possible, in all cases, what is the underlying cause, and then dispute its power to do harm, and at the same time urge the patient to help himself by banishing all doubts and fears of his ultimate recovery. It is very difficult and almost impossible to cure a case where the patient is a stubborn doubter and has no faith in God's power. He must be taught to have implicit faith, and urged to take a brave stand and express his determination to recover from his sickness. When these things are accomplished, the recovery is only a question of time.

The reason why we address disease and bid it depart, as if it was a person and could understand our language, is that experience proves that by so doing the mind becomes more concentrated and gains in power over the disease. If we exhibit any weakness, doubt or want of faith in treating disease, either in ourselves or others, the disease will take a firmer hold and we are sure to fail. Our measure of success will be in proportion to our possession of knowledge and faith. If we doubt our power to heal, we are doubting God's power, for we are a part of Him.

Very often, patients have a great desire to discuss, and will want the healer to make it plain to them how cures can be effected. In these instances it is well to cite them cures that have been effected. Facts will often prove effective when reasoning will fail.

Many persons will say that such a thing is impossible. Arago said, "Outside of pure mathematics, let no man pronounce anything impossible." Everything is possible that is not morally impossible. The impossibilities of one age become the possibilities of the next. The old practitioners in drugs have pronounced it impossible to cure certain cases, but the metaphysical healer has cured many of them.

As a general thing it is wise to avoid discussion with patients, especially if they should have a stubborn disposition. To argue with an obstinate man will only cause him to adhere more closely to his errors. In these cases you can only state results and give facts. Conviction must be left to time.

The adherents of this science must make up their minds to receive some amount of misrepresentation, obloquy and even persecution; but it should always be remembered that he who possesses the truth has a mighty weapon at his command. One cure will have a greater effect upon the minds of most people than all the logical reasoning that can be employed. Then, every case which offers itself for cure is certain to have peculiarities of its own. What will prove effective in one case may fail in another. But there is a cure for everything that is curable, and the practitioner of this science must look upward and onward, never for a moment doubting of ultimate success.

As the mind-cure is really but an exhibition of the

almost omnipotent power which mind has over matter, the student should be careful to master the principles set forth in the chapters of this book.   It is true that we know but little of what mind can do and cannot do; but we know of its mighty power through witnessing its results, and these results are sufficient to inspire us with unbounded confidence and infinite hope.

Even persons who have well studied this system, and practiced it with great success, still confess that there is in it much that they do not understand.   They can neither comprehend nor describe the process of healing. But there are the facts, and no one can dispute these. It is not light cases nor transitory pains alone that are cured, but contagious and hereditary diseases also have been successfully treated.   In some instances these have yielded to a few treatments, but sometimes a long course of treatment has been found necessary.   In Charlestown resides a gentleman, whose eyes were covered with cataracts, and who had been told by one of the most eminent doctors of that city that he would be blind, that nothing could help him.   The patient went to a metaphysical healer, at that time being so blind that he could not read the signs on the street.   After a few weeks of treatment both cataracts had disappeared. Another lady, in Medford, Mass., after a treatment of 125 sittings, was relieved of even a worse blindness. To-day there is scarcely a locality in which cases of cure

are not found. Elsewhere in this book will be found
an account of a few of the many cases which we ourselves have successfully effected.

Too much importance cannot be attached to the influence of the will in effecting cures. Not that the
will itself is a curative agent, but it directs and concentrates forces which are healing agents. It also keeps
off evils. A person, to be a successful healer, either
of himself or others, must believe not only in the power,
but also in the freedom of the will. A believer in the
necessitarian or fatalist doctrine, need never hope to
meet with success. These people believe that every
phenomenon is a cause of its invariable consequent,
and also an effect of its invariable antecedent, and this
antecedent again is an effect of its antecedent, and so
backwards forever. This is the doctrine of necessity.
Necessity is a true doctrine with regard to some things,
and so also is freedom of the will. Two opposites explain and limit each other. You could know nothing
of necessity without there was freedom, no more than
you could know anything of pleasure, except by recognizing it as the opposite of pain. Will is a first cause
—it is self-originating, hence its power. This is one
of the great weapons of the metaphysical healer.
Huxley truly says :—

"That man, I think, has had a liberal education, who
has been so trained in youth, that his body is the ready

servant of his will, * * * whose mind is stored with a knowledge of the great and fundamental truths of nature and the laws of her operations ; one who, no stunted ascetic, is full of life and fire, but whose passions are trained to come to heel by a vigorous will, the servant of a tender conscience ; who has learned to love all beauty, whether of nature or of art, to hate all vileness, and to respect others as himself."

Experience has taught us that although a patient may be fully cured of certain diseases, yet that these diseases will return if the patient is exposed to the old conditions and influences. Hence it is of the highest importance that every person who is cured by this system should receive instructions how to treat himself. Contest with disease is a perpetual battle, for it is ever on the watch, ready to attack the human system, and any fear, any admission of its presence, increases its power. The pitying expressions of friends, such as, "Oh, how sick you look," "You are quite poorly," " You need rest," " You ought to consult a physician," have influences that tighten the chain of disease around patients. Sick persons want cheerful expressions and encouragemeut of every kind.

It will frequently be found that a patient, after one or two treatments, will exhibit symptoms that might lead him to believe that he was in a worse condition than when the treatment began. It should be explained to him that this is but a breaking up of old conditions, and a bringing them to the surface in order to expunge them from the system. Then it must always be borne in mind that moral treatment goes a long way in effecting cures. Upon this subject there are some excellent remarks in a work written by M. Reveillé-Parise on Moral Therapeutics. The author says : " If a patient dies we open his body, rummage among the viscera, and scrutinize most narrowly all the organs and tissues, in the hope of discovering lesions of some sort or another. There is not a small vessel, membrane, cavity or follicle which is not attentively examined—the color, the weight, the thickness, the volume, the alteration—nothing escapes the eye of the studious anatomist. He handles, touches, smells, and looks at everything; then he draws his conclusions one way or another. One thing only escapes his attention—that is, he is looking at merely organic effects, forgetting all the while that he must mount higher up to discover their causes. These organic alterations are observed perhaps in the body of a person who has suffered deeply from mental distress and anxiety ; these have been the energetic cause of his decay, but they cannot be discovered in the laboratory or amphitheatre. Many physicians of extensive experience are destitute of the ability of searching out the mental causes of disease. They cannot read the book of the heart, and yet it is in this book that are inscribed day by day and hour by hour all the griefs, and all the miseries, and all the joys, and all the hopes of man, and in which will be found the most active and incessant principle of that frightful series of organic changes which constitute pathology. This is quite true : whenever the equilibrium of our mental nature is long or very seriously disturbed, we may rest assured that our animal functions will suffer."

It must always be remembered that we are not treating matter, but mind. It is mind affecting mind, and we must aim to bring to our aid all the powers and forces of our souls. We must try to lift up and cherish the spirit, so that it will rise above all discord and inharmony. There must be a perfect understanding of these truths in both healer and patient. There must be a mutual recognition of the influence that mind has over the entire human organization.

In his work on Mental Hygiene, Dr. Sweetzer says, "The influence of the intellect and the passions upon the health and endurance of the human organization has been but imperfectly understood and appreciated in its character and importance by mankind at large. Few, we believe, have formed any adequate estimate of the sum of bodily ills which have their source in the mind. Those of the medical profession, even, concentrating their attention upon the physical, are too prone to neglect the mental causes of disease ; and thus may patients be subjected to the harshest medicines of the pharmacopæia, the true origin of whose malady is some inward sorrow, which a moral balm alone can reach."

Now, although many quotations of a like character from medical works could be given, the healer in this science must not suppose that medical men will endorse metaphysical healing. On the other hand, they are ready with their cries of "quackery," "charlatanism," "humbuggery," and choice terms of a like import. If we can be scolded, ridiculed and frightened from our path, there are numbers ready to perform that task gratuitously. Having put our hands to the plow, we must not look back. If in all cases the healer does not meet with instant success, let him not lose heart. In the path of duty we require patience, kindness, knowledge and hearts of steel, to fight down disease, and also the opposition of those who desire to make a monopoly of treating diseases. We must look upward and onward.

"Give us the nerve of steel,
And the arm of fearless might,
And the strength of will that is ready still
To battle for the right.

Give us the clear, cool brain,
That is never asleep or dozing,
But sparkling ever with bold endeavor
To wake the world from its prosing.

Give us the heart to feel
    The sufferings of another,
And fearless power in the dying hour
    To aid a suffering brother.

Give us the nerve of steel,
    And the arm of fearless might,
And the heart that can love and feel,
    And the head that is always right.

For the foeman is now abroad,
    And the land is filled with crimes—
Let it be our prayer to God,
    'Oh give us the men for the times.' "

The true healer must have something of the missionary spirit in him if he would be successful. And in
view of the fact that disease breeds suffering, poverty
and crime, he can go forth into the world like a true
missionary, scattering blessings amongst mankind. For
these labors the world expects to reward him, so that
at least he may be able to live and labor. And, like a
true missionary, the healer must not fail to take into
account the power of kind words and acts. The worst
way to reform the world is to condemn it, and the
worst way to heal diseases and cure persons of their
errors, is to condemn the individual. The old fable,
wherein the sun and wind disputed as to who would
make the traveler take off his cloak, has still a good
moral for us. The wind blew its hardest, which only
caused the traveler to cling more closely to his garment. But the sun shed its silent rays warmer and
warmer upon the man, until he quietly threw aside his

cloak. Errors are garments that cling more closely to the person when subjected to harsh opposition and up-braiding, but will be quietly thrown aside when touched by the wand of kind treatment. Even the poor drunk-ard may be driven to his cups by censure and contempt-uous words. If erring men are appealed to as if they were men, and not despised brutes, success would more frequently attend the efforts of the reformer. We should never sit in harsh judgment upon the faults and follies of others. The anatomist and sculptor tell us that there is no human being that is perfectly formed. One arm is longer or larger than the other, one side of the body is a little differently shaped from the opposite one. Sometimes the right eye is different from the left, or the nose may be a little awry. We do not find physical perfection anywhere. So in our moral nature we can find defects in every human being. This should teach us charity ; and whether the disease be physical, mental or moral, treatment that is based on sympathy and kindness will prove effective when uncouth and censorious measures will fail. "A soft answer turneth away wrath," when severity will increase the flame. The healer should recollect that his mission is amongst the highest on earth. He is a creator of happiness in others, and when he is conscious of doing this, he him-self will be reaping the highest blessings which it is possible for man to reap on earth.

PROGRESS.

What is progress? This question will be answered according to a man's view of life, and his belief in the meaning and mission of existence. Progress with one man may mean an increase of money; with another a multiplicity of books; while a third may claim that it means the entire freedom of the individual. There is no exact definition to be given to the word progress. Whether in the individual, or in the nation, we can come to the conclusion that true progress does not consist in the accumulation of material wealth. The good Bishop Heber sang :—

> "What though the spicy breezes
> Blow soft o'er Ceylon's isle,
> Though every prospect pleases,
> And only man is vile!"

Let us apply this truth to our state and nation. What though our mines give forth their endless stores! What though the golden grain waves in the breeze! What though our harbors are crowded with ships bearing the flags of every nation, if the pale image of woe, gaunt poverty, and loathsome disease stalk abroad in our streets? Progress cannot simply mean the building of large ships, whether for commerce or for war ; it cannot mean the construction of forts and the mobilization of armies ; it cannot mean even the increase of learning and science, if these are to be confined to a few. No ! no ! True human progress can only be seen and exhibited in the growth of better men and women. Men and women who shall not be discriminated against because of sex or material possessions ; men and women who shall stand equally before the law written and unwritten, especially the latter ; for while in some localities the written law is as free for woman as for man, yet there is a cruel unwritten law in society that condemns woman to eternal infamy for the same act for which there is little or no condemnation for man. We need not enlarge on this subject, as the facts are plain to be seen and read of all men. Progress, to be true, must not be partial and one-sided—it must reach and influence all. The whole tree must grow, and not one branch cultivated at the expense of all the rest.

Progress also consists in the unfolding of the faculties of the human soul. We say unfolding, for the reason that the most ignorant savage is born with the possible faculties of the highest and grandest philosopher that ever appeared on earth. We say " possible faculties," because they are not yet in existence in the primitive man. The embryo—the tendency—are there, but not the things themselves. No person of thought will contend that the oak tree, with its trunk, and branches, and leaves, are in the acorn. But the tendency to become these things is there. So with primitive man ; he does not possess the faculties, even phrenologically speaking, of the cultivated philosopher, and the latter will perform acts that seem to the savage like miracles —he will even regard him as a god. The moral to be learned from these facts, is this : The wisest and most advanced man is still an unfolded and unfolding being. There are faculties and powers in the human soul that our age has not yet witnessed. We have been taught to rely too much for progress upon what are called our reasoning faculties—that is, the faculties that can weigh, measure and draw conclusions from facts and phenomena. But even in our present undeveloped state, there are evidences that men possess higher powers than these reasoning faculties. Kepler was a great mathematician and a reasoning man, but he perceived or conceived of the orbit of Mars, and by a long process of calculation and reasoning he proved the truthfulness of his perception. That perception was simply the exhibition of a power of the mind that has as yet received no name. That power in Kepler's mind grasped at once at a great fact.

To say that it was an ignorant guess, would simply be a display of the grossest ignorance in those who would make the remark. Gilbert perceived that the earth was a great magnet, whose poles were north and south. The truth of this perception has been verified by numerous accurate observations and reasonable experiments. Very many discoveries in all the walks of life have been made by people who did not possess in any marked degree these so-called reasoning faculties, but they possessed a power of seizing hold of the truth. There are other methods of arriving at the secrets of nature than by those of the inductive and deductive processes. As the soul is unfolded it seizes its own. Upon the unfoldment of these other and higher faculties of man, depends our progress. And in proportion as we live in accordance with God's laws, so will the powers of our soul become unfolded; or, in other words, we shall receive the influx of the wisdom and power of the divine spirit.

Let us not mistake mere change for progress, or we shall be like the good woman whose only claim to the title of a progressionist was founded on the fact that every week she changed the position of the furniture in her house. Change of government, of school books, of social relations, or a thousand other things, do not necessarily imply progression. This must be looked for only in the growth and expansion of the soul. Then it is important to know that while we progress in one direction that we do not retrogress in another. It is a lamentable fact that while we are compelled to ad-

mit an improvement in many directions, we have also
to confess that the diseases of man have increased
to an alarming extent. And we should recollect that
disease produces not only weakness and suffering, but
also poverty and crime. It is one of the greatest drag-
chains upon human advancement. Any plan or system of things that will destroy or prevent disease, is so
far an engine of progress. These powers we claim for
metaphysical science. That it possesses these powers,
has been demonstrated in thousands of instances ; so
that the healer and teacher in this science is adding in
no small degree to the progress of mankind. And the
method by which this is done is the only true and lasting one—and just because we do not trust for man's
progress to an improvement merely of his outward circumstances. We begin in the interior. No amount
of paint or powder will put the hue and color of health
upon the cheek. To do this, we must improve internal
man. Put good thoughts into a man's mind and you
will alter the appearance of his countenance, and he,
because of the new thoughts and aspirations within
him, will seek to improve his material surroundings.
In proportion as we improve the mind of man, in proportion as we make the real man healthy, so will a cor-
responding improvement take place in all the depart-
ments of human existence. It is thus we can ascend
the mountain peaks of hope, from whose lofty tops we

behold the dawn of a better day. We can truly exclaim in the words of another :

> "A brighter morn awaits the human day,
> When every transfer of earth's natural gifts
> Shall be a commerce of good words and works;
> When poverty and wealth, the thirst for fame,
> The fear of infamy, disease and woe;
> When war, with its million horrors and fierce hate,
> Shall live but in the memory of Time;
> Who, like a penitent libertine, shall start, look back,
> And shudder at his younger years."

But while we talk of progress, let us not suppose that it is a thing that will come of its own accord. We may pray for it, aspire to it, but we must also labor for it—labor for it with head, heart and hand ; and then we can not only hope for it, but can command it. Great reformers have always been great workers. "Idleness," says the good book, "is the rust of the soul." Let all men and women see that they keep their own souls bright, and they will reflect happiness all down the paths of progress.

> " Work, while yet the daylight shines,
> With a loving heart and true,
> For golden years are fleeting by,
> And we are passing, too.
>
> Wait not for to-morrow's sun
> To beam upon thy way,
> For all that thou can'st call thine own
> Is in this *one to-day*.

Then learn to make the most of life —
  Make glad each passing day;
For time will never bring'thee back
  The chances swept away.

Leave no tender word unsaid—
  Do good while life shall last;
You know the mill can never grind
  With the *water that is past.*"

EDUCATION OF MOTHERS.

The subject of maternity is one of such transcendent importance, not only to the parent, but to the entire race, that it seems marvelous that more has not been written about it. It is true there are difficulties surrounding the treatment of the subject, but no false modesty should teach us to ignore it entirely. Children have rights as well as adults, and have they not a right to sound and healthy constitutions? How many poor children are ushered into the world whose lives, from the cradle to the grave, are one continued journey of sorrow and pain. Herbert Spencer, in his *Treatise on Education*, says: "Seriously, is it not an astonishing fact, that though on the treatment of offspring depend their lives or deaths and their moral welfare or ruin, yet not a word of instruction on the treatment of offspring is ever given to those who will hereafter be parents. Is it not monstrous that the fate of a new generation should be left to the chances of unreasoning custom, impulse or fancy, joined with the suggestions of ignorant nurses and the prejudiced counsel of grandmothers? If a merchant commenced business without any knowledge of arithmetic and book-keeping, we should exclaim at his folly and look for disastrous consequences. Or if before studying anatomy, a man set up as a surgical operator, we should wonder at his audacity and pity his patients. But that parents should begin the difficult task of rearing children without ever having given a thought to the principles—physical, moral or intellectual—which ought to guide them, excites neither surprise at the actors nor pity for their victims. * * * Here are the indisputable facts : that the development of children in mind and body rigorously obeys certain laws, that unless conformed to by parents death is inevitable ; that unless they are in a great degree conformed to, there must result serious physical and mental defects, and that only when they are completely conformed to, can a perfect maturity be reached. Judge then whether all who may one day be parents should not strive with some anxiety to learn what those laws are."

It is a lamentable fact that there is a decrease of healthy maternity among American women, and in some quarters there is an increase of the horrible practice of abortion. These evils must not be laid entirely at the door of woman, for man is in part their instigator. We want to spread knowledge, and create a healthy sentiment on this subject. Even at the expense of not having such fine horses, expert dogs, and fat pigs, we want a stronger, healthier, better class of children. If one or the other must be neglected, we say let the pigs go. Children are brought into the world inheriting the defects, physical and mental, of their parents. If these evils can be prevented, is it not our imperative duty to do it? We shall thereby save the world an immense amount of misery, and also add to the future greatness of mankind. There is not a position in the world so sacred as that of being a mother. It involves duties of the very highest order, and it should be remembered that the child is not the exclusive property of its parents, for as well as belonging to them, it belongs to its country and to its God. It is in the power of the mother, to a very large extent, to mold and make the character of her offspring. Especially is this true of pre-natal condition. At these times, by a wise direction of her own thoughts and will, guided by a thorough knowledge of metaphysical science, she can in a great degree determine the disposition of her child. Fathers, too, should aim at these periods to keep the mother in the happiest and calmest frame of mind. Violent fits of anger, and indeed excitement of every kind, should be avoided. Then in after years, as soon as reason has sufficiently dawned upon the mind, the child should be taught to conquer and treat itself. We have known quite young children to acquire sufficient control over themselves so as to be able to conquer pain. There is no study that is more important to children than the mind-cure. A number of those infantile diseases, such as croup, measles and the like, when not prevented can be very much lessened in their effects and pains, by bringing into exercise by the parent and child the power which the mind has over the body. There are many cases where the dangerous disease of diphtheria has been rendered comparatively harmless by this mental application. Mothers should be taught to know the influence that mind has over matter, and then for the sake of their children they should use that knowledge.

What a race of superior beings might be produced, if mothers would use the power which God has put in their hands. Instead of having wives and mothers in a true sense, society is filled with women who apparently care for nothing more than to make themselves milliners' blocks, and objects of fashion and admiration for the gaping crowd. These remarks are not intended to disparage taste in dress, nor care for the same ; but we desire to lead woman, especially mothers, to higher aims in life, and point them to duties that are of lasting and eternal importance.

SPIRITUALISM.

The mind-cure is the most spiritual of all sciences and systems. We have no desire to enter into a controversy with that large body of citizens calling themselves Spiritualists. We only wish to set ourselves right with them and others by stating that we neither practice clairvoyance nor consult the spirits of the departed when performing our cures. We rely upon the Great Infinite Spirit, God, alone for aid. We ignore alike drugs, magnetism, clairvoyance and the consultation of spirits. We do not deny that some of these things may afford temporary relief, but we doubt their efficacy in effecting permanent cures. We take the position that for effectual cures for disease we must draw from the Divine Fountain of our being, and this we can only do by placing ourselves in harmony with God. It is only by taking this position that we can hope to succeed. While on this earth we are as much spirits as those who have gone beyond the veil. And Spiritualists tell us that the disembodied spirits carry with them the imperfections and errors acquired in this life, and that there, as here, are many unhappy, inharmonious spirits. Of what use, then, is it to call for aid upon those who are like ourselves ? In this life, if we will, we can acquire the knowledge which, by the help of Him "from whom cometh every good and perfect gift," is equal to the cure of all sickness, sin and disease. Let us, then, seek this knowledge—seek it earnestly, in prayer, in faith, in singleness of heart. Christ said, "If thine eye be single, thy whole body shall be full of light." We must neither seek nor work doubtingly, but seek with unclouded vision and an eye single to the discovery of truth as it is, and seeking we shall find, and like the poor woman mentioned in Scripture, we shall be made whole.

We admit that it is sometimes of benefit to lay hands upon a patient's head, for the reason that it concentrates the mind of both healer and patient. We recognize no benefit from the mere contact of the hand, for this would be an admission that there was a curative property in matter. What magnetism is, we know not. By some it is termed a fluid, and by others an essence of mind. Certain it is that it is not mind itself. Neither do we pretend to know what mind is, and it may be we never shall know. There appears to be a reason why we should not have it in our power to define mind. Nothing possesses the power of self-analyzation. A tree, a drop of water, a grain of sand, cannot comprehend nor analyze themselves. These are all forms of matter, and matter cannot investigate nor comprehend itself. Mind investigates matter because it is outside and independent of it. But mind cannot investigate its own essence ; all it can do is to analyze, point out and name its powers and effects.

Again, many Spiritualists claim to have communications from doctors in the spirit world, in which they recommend the use of drugs for effecting cures. Now, as we entirely ignore the use of drugs, of what use would it be to us to call upon these spiritual doctors ? We have quite a sufficient number of M. D.'s of that stripe in this sphere of existence without seeking to call those back who have left their nostrums on earth.

ANTIQUITY OF MIND CURE.

The mind cure is frequently spoken of as that " new method," " the new-fangled theory," and "the modern craze," as if it was an invention of these latter days. The truth is, that the mind-cure is as old as the race. Read the history of any nation, peruse the narratives of all travelers, and you will find that in some form or other a belief in the power of mind over matter, and a practice of mental healing, have always obtained. We are aware that its antiquity does not prove its truthfulness, but it relieves it of the charge that it is a modern invention or discovery. At various times, and amongst all nations, it has appeared under different names. One man has claimed to be a prophet sent by the Lord; another, that he was sent by the angels, or was himself an angel in disguise ; while a third would assert that he possessed a key that would unlock all the mysteries of nature. A still larger number asserted, that while they could perform cures without study or the use of drugs, they knew not whence they derived their power. Now, it is the very simplicity of the method that brings it into disfavor with many persons, especially with those who have pored over books, passed through colleges, and spent mueh time and money in placing them just where they stand. "How can ignorant people effect cures, when they with all their medical skill and know-ledge fail? The thing is absurd, impossible!" they cry. But have not these medical practitioners a diseased no-tion of their own importance? Do they not place an exaggerated estimate upon the value of their learning and facts? Do they not mistake a little information and knowledge for true education in the line of their pro-fession? Watch one of these young students, fresh from his medical college, after obtaining a diploma. If he should have something of the pedant in him, which not unfrequently happens, he will take every op-portunity to use his medical terms in the description of disease. Thus he will stand at the bedside of a sick child, and in answer to the question of the anxious parent regarding the nature of the disease, he will learn-edly stroke his incipient beard and solemnly exclaim, "I observe a few *maculæ* about the face and arms, but the *epidermis* seems to be exclusively involved. There is some febrile movement, and we may rationally ex-pect a *roseola* within a few hours. This case is liable to develop into *rubeola*, with *lachrymation, ozena, an-gina*, and all the other symptoms characteristic of the disease." And pray, most learned doctor, give us an English name for that terrific disease. "Oh, ah, yes;

well, it is the measles!" Thank you, for the modern
name; you can keep the terms of antiquity for use on
some future occasion. There is much in the present
school of medicine that is a huge collection of antiquity,
hewed and plastered into some kind of shape, so as to
make it pass under the name of "the modern school of
medicine." Read the modern works on medicine, and
you find them a conglomeration of terms, of divers and
diverse opinions, and we are struck with a feeling of
awe concerning the things which we do not understand.
How applicable here is the verse—

> " The wise men of Egypt were secret as dummies,
>   And even when they most condescended to teach,
> They packed up their meaning as they did their mummies,
>   In so many wrappers 'twas out of one's reach."

There is, at least, about the mind-cure, the merit of
simplicity. And this, we conceive, should be the merit
of all systems. That which comes to us so mystified,
so wrapped around by high-flown words and phrases,
should always challenge our investigation if not our
doubt. Considering what he has done, the world has
erred in assigning so high a rank to the mere medical
practitioner. The system is a gigantic phantom, and
let the hand of truth and simplicity tear the mask from
its face. Men have invented rules and plans; have
published volumes on the philosophy of life and death;
and their works are replete with quotations and

adorned and dressed in grandiloquent words and phrases; but just here open your Saxon bible and see the purity of diction and the plainness of the language of a Paul, a John and a James. We want this same simplicity in dealing with disease. Let us not ask whether a thing has the air of antiquity about it, or is altogether of modern origin. Let the inquiry be, Is it true, is it effective? That, after all, must be the touchstone. Of course we have nothing to say against learning itself, but we object to its use when wrapped around errors. "The majesty of nature is the curtain of deity; and the light of deity is grace and truth." There is a great deal of stuff and nonsense that for ages have done duty as philosophy. Men need to be taught to trust more and more to their intuitions. It is by these, more than by learning and philosophy, that the world has been carried forward.

> "A few plain instincts and a few plain rules,
> Among the herdsmen of the Alps have wrought
> More for mankind, at this unhappy day,
> Than all the pride of intellect and thought."

Observation and experience have taught us to believe that a few plain rules and a few plain instincts relating to the mind-cure, will do more for mankind than the learned rules of drug-administering medical practitioners.

In modern times considerable attention has been

given to the mind-cure in the United States. Its progress here of late years received its greatest impulse
from Dr. P. P. Quimby, a native of Belfast, Maine.
Of this remarkable man Dr. Dresser, of Massachusetts,
says: "He practiced his system for the cure of the
sick for many years in Maine, and was located in Portland from 1859 to 1865. Dr. Quimby was a man
somewhat peculiar in his make-up. With a mind of
large comprehension, he had a wonderful power of concentration of thought, and he was so extremely practical and mathematical in his mode of reasoning, that it
was with difficulty that he could entertain an opinion,
or any proposition that was not fully demonstrated by
truth. Such a mind, being of an inquiring nature,
would certainly find out the truth of things if it were
possible, before entertaining a mere belief. I witnessed
many of Dr. Quimby's cures, of such cases as paraly-
sis, cancers, tumors, consumption, rheumatism, nervous disorders and other minor complaints. Upon open-
ing a closet door in the doctor's rooms, at one time, I
saw an armful of crutches and canes that had been left
there by people who had come to the doctor in various
crippled conditions, and had gone away without the
need of these supports. It was viewed as a most
speaking sight."

A Boston journal gives an account of the position
and advancement of the science in that city:

"In Boston there are four schools of this system, and all of these hold as their fundamental idea that disease does not come from God, and that He has nothing to do with its perpetuation, but that it is one of the errors of man which can be cured by truth ; the application of this truth is not by faith, but by an intelligent understanding. The schools, however, disagree in regard to later developments, some claiming to be farther advanced than the others. Of the few heads of these schools, one—Dr. Evans, now residing in East Salisbury—is a venerable gentleman of 60 odd years of age, who was formerly a clergyman for twenty-five years before he visited Dr. Quimby as a patient twenty-one years ago, and following which he left preaching and practiced healing the sick, employing rubbing and manipulating as a part of his system. Another leader and head of a school is Mrs. Eddy, who resides on Columbus avenue, and who was a patient with Quimby twenty-two years ago. Her assumed title is Christian Scientist, and her followers bear the same name. A third is Dr. E. J. Arens, residing at Union Park, who practices and teaches under the name of metaphysician. The fourth leader is Dr. J. A. Dresser, residing on Columbus avenue, a pupil of Dr. Quimby, who follows out his teacher's system, pure and simple. Besides these four practitioners, there are about a dozen others who practice the mind-cure as a profes-

sion, and who teach to classes of young and old the
methods of curing. Generally, free instruction is given
once a week to all who will come. Among those who
have attended these lectures are many Bostonians,
who, though decidedly averse to having the fact pub-
licly known, for fear of ridicule, yet are imbued with
faith—some with a little, some with a great deal—in the
truth of the system, and who often practice at their
homes on the husband, father or son who happens to
believe that he is afflicted with a headache, toothache,
or sore finger. And they claim success in curing."

Of Dr. Quimby, we remember when quite young, of
his going round the country effecting cures that were
looked upon by many as being miracles. There was
an anecdote told of him, that we think has not before
found its way to print :—When near Portland, Maine,
he called at a house, to the inhabitants of which he was
a stranger. He found a middle-aged man seated on
the verandah, and asked if he could obtain a drink of
water. The man replied that he could, but as his people
were away, and he was lame from rheumatism, that he
would have to help himself. Quimby replied, that he
did not think he was lame, and believed he could walk.
The man said, " It is a long time since I have been able
to walk, or even to move about, except by the aid of
crutches." Quimby replied, " I realize that you can
walk ; give me your hand." He took the man by the

hand, and caused him to walk back and forth on the verandah ; and before he left the lame man had no use for his crutches, and could walk as well as he ever could. When his people returned, greatly to their astonishment, they found him walking in the garden. He asked Quimby for his name, but this he refused to give, for the reason that he hated notoriety. He would "do good by stealth, and blush to find it fame." Of such stamp was this modern apostle of the mind-cure.

There can be no doubt that those cases that have come down to us from old times, wherein it is claimed that the Lord sent down his servants from Heaven to make cures, have been made through the influence of mind acting upon mind. India, China, Japan, Egypt, Syria, even our old Scandinavian mythology, are rich with accounts of cases that have yielded to this silent, unseen influence, when all other means have failed. Fortunately, we have both antiquity and modern times on our side. But what has been done is only to be taken as an earnest of what we can do.

> " I doubt not through the ages one increasing purpose runs,
> And the thoughts of men are widening with the process of the suns."

EFFICACY OF PRAYER.

What is prayer? "It is the heart's sincere desire, uttered or unexpressed." In view of all that we have previously advanced, how much can we reasonably hope from the employment of prayer? On this subject mankind can be readily divided into two classes, namely, those who expect too much from praying, and those who flatly deny its utility. The monks of old sang, *Laborare est orare*—"To labor is to pray." This is worthy to be remembered by those who would trust everything to prayer. There are good prayers, and there are vain, foolish, and even malicious prayers. The time has come when it behooves our churches to look a little more closely than they have hitherto done at the uses and power of prayer. If there is any one time more than another that it is wrong to take God's name in vain, it is when men pray to Him simply to have their own selfish ends answered, or that they may receive some benefit or blessing which they are too indolent to labor for. Many, very many, prayers are simply utterances of conventional blasphemy. Two monarchs go to war, both believing in the same God, and they cause prayers to be said in all of their respective churches for the success of their respective arms. Are these people in a true sense praying to God at all ? Are they not selfishly and savagely ejaculating one against the other ? Two adjoining farmers pray to God ; one wants dry weather and the other rain. Each wants his selfish ends answered without regard to the other's welfare. Are not all such prayers better left unsaid ? Nay, are they not wicked prayers ? What these people really need is a truer knowledge of their own relations and duties—and higher, nobler and grander conceptions of Almighty God. The Master told us to pray to the Father in these words : "Thy will be done on earth as it is in heaven."

Right here, those who do not believe in prayer will say : "But will not God do His will without our praying to him ?." We answer that God and the Universe will do that which is right and proper for us when we supplicate aright. Prayer alone is a useless thing, but prayer with work in the right direction is a combination of power that nothing can resist. There is not a man on earth who does not, at some time or other, pray. An aspiration is a prayer ; and there never yet was a man who aspired to, and prayed for, a good and needed thing, that was not drawn nearer to that goodness, and its attainment thereby made more easy. Let the inebriate pray fervently and earnestly to become a sober man, and he will soon find his efforts and work in the direction of his prayer. Let a false, useless, worthless man truly pray to become manly, and true, and good, and his prayer will act like a trumpet calling his energies to arm and to battle. So that in these directions prayer is of incalculable benefit. But we do not limit its uses to this one power. May not a true prayer be an appeal to a law, or to the invoking of a law? We know not. We find that our own intense desires are often communicated to other minds, even without our uttering a word. We know not by what process this is done, but we know it to be a fact. And there are millions of well attested facts in existence showing that prayers have brought forth fruit. Just how far the power of prayer extends, and the effort, which is something different, begins, we cannot tell. But we know that there are two distinct forces, though we cannot draw the line of demarcation; just as we know that there are distinct things in hill and valley, though we cannot draw the line between them. Let no man scoff at prayer; he may sometimes say, "I do not know enough to believe, and I do not know enough to ridicule." So far as prayer has influence in the mind-cure, it may, for aught we know, serve to concentrate and direct the needed curative force. But we cannot hope for success until we acquire a knowledge of God's laws and how to apply them. Let us never forget that all good work is a good prayer.   There are cases where mere words are but a mockery, and in these cases good deeds are the only effective prayers.   A prayer offered to a hungry, famishing man, would not supply his wants. What he would need would be the prayer of the Good Samaritan.

" Give him a lift, don't kneel in prayer,
    Nor moralize with his despair ;
The man is down, and his great need
    Is ready help, not prayer or creed.

'Tis time when the wounds are washed and healed
    That the inward motive be revealed;
But now, whate'er the spirit be,
    Mere words are but a mockery.

One grain of aid just now is more
    To him than tomes of saintly lore ;
Pray, if you must, within your heart,
    But give him a lift, give him a start.

The world is full of good advice,
    Of prayers, and praise and preaching nice;
But the generous souls who aid mankind,
    Are scarce as gold and hard to find.

Give like a Christian, speak in deeds,
    A noble life's the best of creeds,
And he shall wear a royal crown
    Who gives them a lift when they are down."   '

Love, prayer, action, are the three graces that must go hand in hand on the road of humanity.   Each left alone, will effect little or nothing.   When each is genuine, it will link itself to the others.   These constitute the hope, the happiness, and the progress of the human race.

PERSONAL EXPERIENCE.

When we began to investigate the claims of this science, we did so with the determination of making our researches thorough. We had previously investigated a number of the isms of the day, but we could find no resting place, and were mentally starving for something to believe in and feed upon. The more we studied and thought, the more brightly the light dawned upon us, and we soon found that the mind-cure was capable of doing all that its most ardent advocates claimed for it. About the first practical truth that we had of its efficacy was when we were cured of a case of diphtheria in about twenty minutes by a lady who had had some experience in the science. We then commenced studying the system. Some time after this we called upon a lady who was suffering from neuralgia, and had been suffering from the same excruciating pain at intervals for three or four years' past. Periods of suffering would afflict her sometimes for seven or eight days together. When we called upon her she had been suffering for about three days, and during all that time had been deprived of sleep. On her chest and sides were numerous mustard plasters, which had afforded her no relief. We told her that if she would follow directions, and would remove her plasters, we would treat her for her complaint. This she did, saying that she would do anything to get rid of her pain. We then gave her a treatment for about fifteen minutes, at the end of which time she felt almost free from pain, and expressed astonishment at the result. That evening she retired to sleep early, and slept till 9 o'clock the next morning, and rose refreshed and perfectly free from pain. When we called upon her she expressed great surprise at the cure. We then gave her instructions how to treat herself. The pain was entirely removed, and she has repeatedly said to friends that she would not part with her knowledge for a million of dollars. This was about the first cure we effected, and this act gave us more confidence in the mind-cure than all the reasoning in the world could have done. This case, we may say, was our starting point as a practitioner. From that time to this we have met with almost unvarying success. Another extraordinary case that we will mention, is that of a lady who had been suffering for about three years from a complication of diseases peculiar to the female system. She had the advice and experience of several eminent physicians of San Francisco, had also placed herself under the charge of magnetic healers, but in every case without receiving any permanent benefit. She had given up all hope of ever getting well. On paying her a visit, we found her in bed, in a desponding mood. By treatment, argument and entreaty, we induced her to get up and walk up to our rooms, where we gave her further treatment. These treatments were continued every day for a week. During this week she admitted that she had walked more than she had done for years past. From the time we gave her the first treatment she never had occasion, through sickness, to return to her bed. In about three weeks after this, she had perfectly recovered. We taught her the science, and she at once commenced treating and teaching others. She is now a happy and useful woman.

Another case was that of a lady of about fifty years of age, who had been salivated when young, from the effects of which she had never recovered. Physicians to whom she had applied, had informed her that her internal organs had become so much impaired, that that there were no hopes of her recovery, and that all she could do would be to make herself as comfortable as possible. After two weeks' treatment we restored her to health and happiness.

A daughter of this lady came to us to be treated for curvature of spine and some nervous trouble. This was another case that physicians had abandoned. After about fourteen treatments she was completely restored to health.   This young lady learned the science, and is now practicing the same.   She forwarded to us a few words concerning her own case, with full liberty to publish the same.   The following is the communication :

No. 8 Bond Street,

San Francisco, June 1st, 1884.

I had been suffering from spinal disease, caused from a fall when a child.   Also from torpid liver, indigestion and general nervous debility.   I had been treated by different physicians, who would patch me up for a short time, but then I would get back in my old plan again, when I heard of Mrs. J. A. Root, who practiced by metaphysical science the art of healing.   I was treated by her, and gradually all my pains and disagreeable feelings left me.   I pronounce myself cured, and have learned the science.

Miss M. E. Shephard.

Another case was that of a lady, who called upon us with her husband.   She had been suffering for several years with pains in her stomach.   She had applied to several physicians, who had given her no relief. She had also tried various remedies prescribed for her by sympathizing friends, but without avail.   On the morning of her visit to us, she had been suffering excruciating pains, and was hardly able to move about.

On questioning her, we learned that about six years ago she had eaten something that contained poison. After a few minutes of treatment she acknowledged to feeling better. The blood in her veins began to circulate freely. We gave her in all five treatments, and she was completely restored to health. The following is a copy of a letter received from her:

QUINCY, PLUMAS CO., CAL.,
May 11, 1884.

MRS. J. ANDERSON ROOT :

Dear Friend :—I have suffered from troubles of the stomach and head, also nervous trouble, for several years, until you gave me the first treatment, which improved me greatly. I have taken five treatments, and feel well and strong.

If this will be of any benefit to you or others, you may use it. Gratefully yours,

MRS. W. J. EDWARDS.

The following is another testimonial received from one of our patients :

622 ELLIS STREET,
San Francisco, March 26, 1884.

After suffering a number of years from neuralgia, and thinking my case hopeless, my attention was at last drawn to the new metaphysical science as practiced by Mrs. J. Anderson Root, of San Francisco, and now

I am happy to say to the public that I was entirely cured by that lady in one treatment.

MINNA FRANCES.

We will further add that since treating Mrs. Frances we were called upon to pay a visit to her house, and found her son, a youth of fifteen years of age, suffering severely from an attack of pneumonia. We at once gave him a treatment, which threw him into a profuse perspiration. He went to bed and slept soundly, and after awakening, he was restored to health. This is another fact, which is worth a whole volume of reasoning.

We add a further testimonial of the efficacy of mind-cure :

No. 707 POST STREET,
San Francisco, April 26th, 1884.

MRS. J. ANDERSON ROOT :

I desire to say, for the benefit of the public and the advancement of the mind-cure, that I was suffering from what was supposed to be an incurable malady. I was treated by several popular physicians, and also by magnetic healers, but with little benefit. In a fortunate moment you came to me, and after a few treatments I was restored to health. My cure seemed to me miraculous ; I had given up all hopes of recovery.

Since that time I have learned the science, and am

now practicing successfully, and God helping me I shall labor faithfully in the field of love and truth.

Mrs. E. S. Hill.

We have given the above testimonials, not for the purpose of parading our own skill, but as so many facts, proving beyond a doubt that the mind-cure proved effective where the skill of the best medical men, aided by the power of all the drugs in their pharmacopœia, has failed.

INSANITY.

No man has as yet been enabled to draw the line of demarcation between sanity and insanity. One learned writer asserts that "all men are at times tinged with insanity." It is a common remark, upon speaking of something that is beyond dispute, that "it is as plain as your nose on your face." But though the nose is plain enough on the face, yet it is not possible to draw the line where the nose joins the face. We do not, however, argue from our inability to do this that they are not two distinct things. So, from our inability to draw the line between sanity and insanity, we must not contend that there are not two distinct conditions of mind. The use of one term to express a condition, necessarily implies the opposite. Otherwise, we are all either sane or we are all insane. Certain it is that there is always much in the world that is termed insanity that is only a high and advanced form of sanity. Arkwright, the inventor, was believed by his neighbors, and by his own wife, to be an insane man, simply because he contended that he could invent a machine that would do the work of many men.

Our own Fulton, who ran the first steam vessel, was believed by very many intelligent persons to be insane —and for no other reason than that he had notions that were contrary to and in advance of their own. All up and down history we find that nearly every man who had ideas, whether in poetry, art, science, mechanics, or religion, that were in advance of the ideas of those around him, was adjudged by the community as being insane. How, then, can advocates of the mind-cure be surprised if now and then they are dubbed "crazy people?" That which is the insanity of one age often becomes the admired sanity of another. After all, we only make approximations as to what is, and what constitutes insanity. Some persons are deemed insane on one point, and some on another, while others are insane at one period of time and at other moments are deemed perfectly rational and intelligent. Medical men can give us no rules for guidance that are accepted as final in any court of justice, as to what constitutes insanity. It is purely a matter of opinion.

Insanity has many causes. One man becomes insane through the loss of money ; the loss of friends, of children ; the use of opiates and narcotics ; fright, starvation, and many other things and conditions have reduced thousands upon thousands to that condition which we all agree to call insane. That it is in some cases inherited, is placed beyond a doubt. Esquirol found among 1,375 lunatics 337 unquestionable cases of hereditary transmission. Guislain and others regard that at least one out of every four insane persons inherit the disease. Dr. Morel gives an account of a family in which he attended four brothers. Their grandfather had died insane, while their father had no powers of concentration, but would be constantly changing his mind from one thing to another. Of these four children one was a maniac; another was afflicted with melancholy madness; the third had suicidal intentions; the fourth was extremely timorous and suspicious.

Now, there must be something rotten about our boasted civilization, or else about our physical and mental doctors, when this scourge is a thousand times more distinguishable among civilized than among un-civilized nations. And there must be something still more rotten about the system which permits the huddling together in localities of hundreds and thousands of these unfortunates, and then learnedly calling it treatment of the insane. Our asylums are but institutions for the preservation of insanity. The words written over the entrance to Dante's Inferno, "Leave all hope behind, ye who enter here," should be inscribed over the gates of every asylum in the land. How few of these unfortunates are restored to health and their friends. Asylums are medical institutions for the in-

oculation of insanity.   We have as yet had no opportunity of fairly trying to cure a case of insanity, but
when conditions can be made favorable, we shall certainly try the experiment without fear of the result.
We hope to see the time when the mind-cure will be
given as fair a trial for treating the insane, as is now
given to a system of close confinement and drugs.
That the soul itself can become insane, is, from our
standpoint, an utter impossibility—that it can have its
origin in matter, is to us simply an absurdity ; and the
men of the lance and the probe have never yet pre-
tended that they have discovered its cause in the disarrangement of the physical structure.   In what direction, then, shall we look for it ?   We answer, in the
unconscious mind, or in the disarrangement of that
condition of vitality and sensation that is brought about
by the influence of mind upon matter.

NECESSITY OF CONDITIONS.

All through the pages of this book we have sought to make the widest possible distinction between mind and matter. We have also aimed to show that the invisible is the only real and permanent thing in the Universe. All the mighty changes that are forever and forever going on around us are simply the results of invisible mind, which in one direction or another is stamping itself upon dead, dull, inert matter. Hold in your hand a watch, and with its springs, levers, wheels, brightly polished, finely adorned metals, it is a thing of beauty—a thing of life. What has produced it ? Mind ! That mechanism was once dull, shapeless, inactive matter. As a watch, it owes its existence to mind. So it is with our houses, ships, palaces, monuments, machines, temples, and all things that entitle us to the name of civilization. A man that we call a sculptor, comes along with the unseen image of the beautiful imprinted on his unseen mind—he finds a senseless, ill-shapen block of marble, and upon this he carves the image of his mind. Behold the statue! What made it? Mind ! Turn in what direction you please—put your question in any form you desire, and the answer will still come to you—it is mind! mind! that produces these mighty results. What is it that animates, moves and controls these muscles of the body—that makes the eye to see, the ear to hear, and the tongue to speak? It is mind, mind, everywhere. Watch the silent stars at night; hear the rushing of the cataract; the booming of the ocean; see the mighty forests, the gladsome flowers, and the countless forms of life that everywhere prevail, and ask what produces all these? The answer again comes—it is the mind!

> "It warms in the sun, refreshes in the breeze,
> Glows in the stars, and blossoms in the trees;
> Lives through all life, extends through all extent,
> Spreads undivided—operates unspent."

Now, although we thus attribute everything to mind, and give to it a creative, a remedial and curative power, let it not be supposed that we entirely ignore the necessity of complying with conditions in order to obtain and preserve our bodies and minds in a healthy state. To take such a stand as that would very justly expose us to the charge of fanaticism or insanity. Undoubtedly there are conditions which we now, in our imperfect state, have to comply with, that by-and-by we shall entirely ignore. As knowledge increases, and as mind is brought into play, we can dispense with conditions which we are now compelled to comply with. We had at one time to comply with the conditions, sails, winds and currents, in order to cross the ocean. To-day we have rendered these conditions unnecessary. At one time we had to comply with conditions, ink and paper, to send a message to a friend ; but unseen mind calls to our aid an invisible agent, and lo! our old conditions are put aside. And Utopian as it may seem to many, we believe that the age will come when even the telegraph will be superseded as a condition of forwarding messages. Who will dare to limit the power of mind! We shall one day exclaim, "Old things are passed away; behold all things are become new." There was a time when men could not exist at the bottom of the ocean, but now, with a simple diving apparatus, they can spend hours under water without the slightest injury to themselves. Thus, one by one man is overcoming conditions, and putting them aside as useless or harmless.

These views will apply to man and his conditions of health. There are things and conditions relating to man and his organism that it is now absolutely necessary for us to comply with, which by-and-by, when we come to know more and more of mind and its powers, that we can completely ignore. Until that time arrives it would be worse than folly for us not to inculcate the necessity of observing conditions, and of complying with their requirements.

Suppose by the power of this science we should win

a man from his inordinate craving for strong drink, we do not contend that if he return again to his cups that the drink will have no effect upon him—we do not even say that he will never thereafter feel a return of his appetite for liquor. But we do say, and there are many cases to prove the truth of our saying, that we can remove that appetite and give him the knowledge which, if he will apply, he can become the master of his appetite, and he shall never again become its slave. He can by the power of his own mind prevent himself from falling into his slavish condition, and this is a grander and more effective weapon to put into his hands than the strongest chemical argument that can be adduced. The habits of the inebriate and some kindred cases are peculiar for this reason, that these persons know better than they act—they sin against knowledge. These cases, for this very reason, require a different kind of treatment. There are cases, as everybody knows, of sickness and disease that are the results of sheer ignorance, and the patient's mind has only to be directed to the case, and the requisite treatment supplied by the healer, for relief or cure to be speedily brought about. We do not advise persons to rush into miasmatic and malarious districts in order to prove that the mind-cure can prove effective in the treatment of fever and ague. We have not yet learned that the allopath recommends this course, in order to prove the power of arsenic or quinine. We know that the sanitary condition of our cities and houses everywhere requires to be improved. Ventilation in sleeping apartments, especially, is in the worst possible condition. Food is eaten that never ought to be taken into the stomach. The results are disease, suffering and premature death. Against these things we wage an uncompromising war. Our weapons are not drugs, for this would be but putting one devil into the system to drive another out.

These are conditions that we protest against. We also, for the sake of our common nature, protest against the habits of some medical men in telling their patients that their cases are serious, that such an organ is diseased, that the functions of another are disturbed, and another almost gone. This practice is as dangerous, if not more so, than the administration of drugs. To our knowledge, many persons' lives have been shortened by the remarks of these medical men. They thus create a condition worse than that in which they find the sufferer. Experience will bear us out when we say that the most successful of medical practitioners have been those who have had the most cheerful dispositions, and have administered the fewest drugs. This is only another way of saying, the less poison and the more mind-treatment the patient receives, the more sure is his recovery.

So far from our ignoring conditions, we teach persons

to get out of bad conditions as speedily as possible—to expose themselves to those conditions as little as possible ; but when through exposure, neglect or ignorance, disease is contracted, let them not add disease to disease by the use of poisonous drugs.

At the moment of writing this, the cholera, supposed to be of the Asiatic type, has made its appearance in Marseilles, Toulon, Arles, and several other cities and towns in France. Whatever may be the immediate cause of this disease, it is certain that the most skillful physicians cannot agree upon the point. It seems, however, to be conceded that fright kills more persons than the disease itself. Many have become insane through fear, while others have committed suicide. This is another proof of the effect of the mind upon the body. A public journal, in commenting on this subject, says : "There is little if any danger of a healthy man with a strong mind being affected with the epidemic. It is fear that causes some persons to contract the disease, and it is fear that kills others." So that, in concluding this chapter on conditions, we remark that by far the greatest of all conditions in warding off disease of any kind, and in curing the same, is the condition of the mind itself. This is both a bulwark and a weapon. Let all persons seek to use it. An even mind and a firm and resolute will are worth all the drugs in the universe for the prevention and cure of disease of any and all descriptions.

QUESTIONS AND ANSWERS.

It is hoped and believed that the following information, put into the form of questions and answers, will be of considerable use to the students of metaphysical science, and impress upon their minds certain facts and truths which it is important for them to know.

WHAT IS GOD?

God is the divine intelligence that creates, upholds and governs all things. He is self-existent—had no beginning and can have no ending. He is the great Fountain of Mind from which all other minds derive power and intelligence. He is not separated from the work of His hands, but "lives through all life and extends through all extent." Neither is he separated from man, but will at all times hearken to the cry of those who seek Him aright. The idea that God made this world as a mechanic makes a machine and sits apart to watch its operations, is a crude idea and worthy only of barbarous ages. God is in His works. He is never idle, but is ever breathing the breath of life into and through all animate things. As a single lamp will light a million tapers without being in the least diminished, so countless billions of souls emanate from God without diminishing His power.

WHAT IS TRUTH?

In one aspect truth is, as Locke remarks, an affair of language. Two persons witness an event; one uses language and relates the event just as it occurred, but another uses words that convey things that are not like the occurrence. The one, we say, speaks the Truth, the other speaks falsely. The word fact is often used erroneously for the word truth. It is time to insist upon the proper use of these words. A fact is a thing done, and a thing that exists or has existed. Thus it is a fact that such a man as Washington existed; it is a fact that grass is green; it is a fact that thousands were killed at the battle of Waterloo; but we cannot properly call these facts truths. In brief, we may say that facts are things as they exist, and occurrences; truth is the exact relating of these things as they exist and occur. But a truth may also be a principle, an inherent quality, a tendency—a something that has never taken place or been acted out. Friar Bacon is said to have invented gunpowder; let us rather say that he was not an inventor, but a discoverer of qualities or principles inherent in certain chemical substances. He found that if nitre, charcoal and sulphur were mixed in certain proportions, that the mixture would form a certain compound called gunpowder. Now, if Friar Bacon had not discovered the making of gunpowder, would it not have been true that these mixtures would still have formed that compound? If their relations had not been discovered for 500 years hence, would it not still have been true that they would have made gunpowder? The same things can be said of dynamite, or any other chemical compound. Principles are truths, whether they are carried out into fact or not. This is also true of moral and mental principles. They are all equally truths, whether man applies them or not. The Bible says, that "a soft answer turneth away wrath;" but if all men up to this date had given harsh answers to wrath, would not that saying still have been true? Read the Beatitudes in the Fifth Chap. Matthew—they are eternally true, whether man acts upon them or not. Their truth does not depend upon the point of their being exhibited in an act.

Here, then, we see that truth is a different thing from a fact. It exists before the fact, and is independent of it. Truth is an emanation from God, and whether man discovers these truths or not, or whether he acts upon the truth when discovered, or declines to do so, it is still eternal truth. It is safe to say that principles, or the rays of truth, are streaming in every direction around us, and in proportion as we discover them and act upon, so do we become truthful and Godlike.

WHAT IS CREATION?

It is the outward and visible manifestation of an inward creating intelligent power. It is the precipitation of the divine mind. It is the unfolding and blossoming of the thoughts of God. So far as the creation of this earth is concerned, it had a beginning; but so far as the boundless universe is concerned, it had no beginning. Creation is a river that has flowed eternally—it is flowing now, and will forever continue so to do.

The work of Creation is never finished, for God creates for ever and for ever. Evolution is not opposed to creation, but rather adds strength and wonderment to it. Assume, if you choose, that many of the forms of life which we see were evolved from a single germ, it only increases our wonderment that a germ should possess so many amazing potentialities. This only adds grandeur to the eternal Creator for having so marvelous a power as to endow a small thing with such wonderful unfolding powers and possibilities.

Astronomy proves to us that worlds are still in process of formation, and are being fitted for life and the abode of man. Nature is more than it seems to us—more than this world, which is but a small bubble floating on a shoreless sea of space. If any person thinks that this earth is the only place in the universe that is fitted up for the abode of intelligent beings, then that person accuses Nature and God of having created countless worlds and suns in vain. As soon as men learn that this earth is but one, and by no means the largest body moving round the sun, and that worlds and suns are infinite in number, then their ideas of Creation will expand, and they will have more exalted notions of God, the Creator.

WHAT IS MIND?

Mind is the exact opposite of matter. It has a dynamic power over matter. As clay is in the hands of the potter, so is matter in the control of mind. It is not matter that fashions and controls mind, but it is mind that shapes and governs matter. Undoubtedly there are laws governing mind, but as yet we know nothing of them. We see and feel its power—we know of its many and varied operations ; but we do not know all that it can do, nor yet what it cannot do. It is immortal in its essence. It is an emanation from God. It is that which receives and retains impressions both consciously and unconsciously, so that we may be said to have a conscious and unconscious mind. When harmonious impressions are made upon the mind the results are health and happiness ; when those impressions are discordant they produce pain and disease. How careful then we should be in subjecting ourselves to impressions.

WHAT IS MATTER?

It is that which possesses neither feeling, intelligence, force, nor power of motion. See, side by side, the living, warm, active man, and the motionless corpse. The one lifts an arm, it gestures, it speaks, it feels, its numerous senses are keenly alive to external things. But the other! Speak to it, move it, dissect it, but it hears not, it feels not, it manifests no thought. Why not ? There are all the organs—it has a brain, nerves, muscles, the same as the other, but it is only matter. That which alone can feel, think and act, is not there. What language can make it plainer that matter, even when organized, has in itself no feeling, motion or intelligence. All that we know of matter is by certain properties, such as form, size, color, weight and so forth. So far as the eye is concerned we have only a surface knowledge of it. Take a cube of wood into the hands, and you see its various sides. Cut it in two, and in each piece you still see only the surface of the parts. And however often you may divide it, it is still surface, and surface only that you behold. However large or small the piece may be, this fact still holds true of it. Now, though matter is considered by some to be the only substantial and lasting thing in the universe, yet, in truth, it is restless, fleeting, and unsubstantial. It is for ever and for ever undergoing change. The globules of water in ocean, lake and river; the particles of the impalpable ether; the atoms of the granite mountain, are never at rest, but are silently changing—imperceptibly to the eye it may be, but still they are never at one-millionth part of a second the same as they are at the immediately preceding part. That which we call decay is only chemical change, and this decay overtakes all things. Everything of which we have knowlenge or can conceive, is eternally growing, decaying, changing. The eye sees the chains of mountains, the firm rock that for thousands of years hath withstood the lashings of mighty waves, but these are ever changing.

> " Like the baseless fabric of a vision,
> The cloud-capped towers, the gorgeous palaces,
> The solemn temples, the great globe itself,
> Yea, all which it inherits shall dissolve,
> And, like an unsubstantial pageant fade,
> Leave not a rack behind."

As the clay is in the hands of the potter, so is visible matter in the power of invisible mind.   And while this matter passes away, mind endureth for ever.   What has been said respecting matter has not been to deny its existence ; to do this, as an author remarks, would be an act of lunacy.   We are only desirous of showing that the common notion about matter is an erroneous one.

WHAT IS EVIL?

Evil is an opposing force to that which is good, but it is not an equal force with goodness.   Some persons call evil undeveloped good.   If so, undeveloped good is evil, and often for the hour or the day it has more than the force of that which is good.   But evil is not lasting ; it passeth away.   But truth and goodness possess an inherent force and immortality of their own. Evil cannot destroy evil ; this can only be done by truth.   Darkness cannot banish darkness ; this can only be done by light.   Man possesses the power of overcoming evil by using the weapon of Truth, which God has placed in his mind and soul.   Evil is unharmony.   The word harmony is thought by many to be restricted to sound. Sir Thomas Browne says : " There is a music in beauty, and the silent note which Cupid

strikes is far sweeter than the sound of an instrument."
Byron speaks of "the mind, the music breathing from
the face." When we speak of the music of the spheres,
we mean the harmony of form and motion. Physical
harmony in the human body means a just and harmonious relation between all its parts and forces. Take
the two extremes of heat and cold. Either of these in
excess will destroy the body, but when they are in a
harmonious relation, the body is in health. The same
may be said of labor and rest.

When we act in accordance with law we are in harmony with it. We are one with it. The patri-
arch Jacob was said to be "one with God."—that
is, he acted in harmony with the laws of God, and
so are we "one with God" when we act in harmony
with His physical and moral laws. When we do not
act in harmony with these, then so far our acts are
evil. The aim of the mind-cure is to destroy evil by
producing harmony, and to bring every sinful man back
to the laws of God.

Further, the would-be definition that "evil is undeveloped good" is apt to lead people astray. Others
have defined evil as being "nothing in itself—a mere
negation of positive good, the same as cold is in itself
nothing but a mere absence of heat." This analogical
reasoning is often false, and should always be intelli-
gently used. If by saying that cold is only the absence

of heat it is meant to imply that it is not a positive force, then the assertion is plainly false. In itself it may be a nothing, or a mere negation, but it is such a negation, when in a state with something else, as to have all the force of that which is a positive. If cold is nothing, cold air, cold water, cold earth are positive things. Cold air, sweeping over a lake, will cover its surface with ice. Cold air will, if intense enough, destroy life. The air warmed by the rays of the sun, sweeping over the lake, will melt that ice. Again the air becomes cold, and again the ice is formed. Are not both agents positive in producing positive results? So with good and evil. Call evil, if you will, a mere negation, or only the absence of good, but when that evil is combined with force it has all the power for the time being of positive good. The arm, when outstretched by the force of goodness, will minister peace and comfort to the suffering and needy; but the same arm, when uplifted by the force of evil, will bring suffering, and even death.

WHAT IS TIME?

Perhaps there is no word in more constant use than the word "time." How few who ask themselves what it means. Mention the word time and the eyes are instantly turned to the clock. But if all the clocks and watches were put out of existence, if all the hour-glasses and sun-dials were destroyed, if the earth should be consumed by fire, the sun cease to shine, and every particle of matter resolved into impalpable ether, time would still exist—would still follow on as it ever has done and must ever continue to do. Time is not a force—it is only a condition in which forces exist and operate. It is a common saying that "time teaches him who has no teacher"; but it is not time that teaches us, but the events, the facts, the experiences and troubles that occur in time that make an impression upon us and teach us. Time, as we have before said, is not a force in itself, and can produce nothing and can exert no in-fluence. Schopenhauer very finely says: "Time flies over things, but leaves no trace upon them." Causes operate in time, and produce the changes which are erroneously attributed to time, as if the latter was a force in itself. Cities have become deserts, luxurious soils and dwelling-houses and temples have been buried deeply beneath burning sands. Where now the icy regions hold fast in their embrace eternal solitude and silence, geology proves to us that the most gorgeous plants once thrived and blossomed in thermal regions of light, life and beauty. See the aged man whose head is silvered with straggling hairs; mark the furrows in his cheek ; look upon the crumbling Parthenon ; the Roman monuments falling to dust; the massive and lofty Pyramids silently but surely shrinking away, and ask if it is time that is the operator. No, it is the sun, the rain, the wind, the laws of nature, which are never idle, that are working these changes. Time is the element, the condition in which these forces operate ; but time has no force of its own—it is not a force at all. We pretend to measure time by clocks and watches, but these things after all are but mechanical instruments made to perform certain revolutions ; and by their agreement one with another we are enabled to regulate our own movements one with another ; but these instruments are not time itself, nor the true measure of time. Let a man suffer intense pain, let his mind be held in suspense in anticipation of something, and what we call five minutes is to him an hour. So far as time is related to us, and so far as we can measure its duration, we can only do this by the soul—by the intensity of the unseen life within us.

> " We live in deeds not years—in thoughts not breaths—
> In feelings, not in figures on a dial.
> Count time by heart-throbs; he lives most who feels most,
> Thinks the noblest, acts the best."

Time is neither a force nor a thing—it can do nothing of itself. Time is a condition in which the soul acts.

WHAT IS RELIGION ?

Many answers have been given to this question. According to Quatrefages, religion is a "belief in beings superior to man, and capable of exercising good or evil influences upon his destiny ; and the conviction that the existence of man is not limited to the present life, but that there remains for him a future beyond the grave." Whatever definition we may try to give it will be found more or less incomplete. The metaphysical healer, in dealing with the Bible, gives to it a spiritual significance, while many look at it entirely from a materialistic standpoint. It matters not so much to us what is religion, as what are religious acts. Christ went about healing the sick, and if we do the same we know that we are thus far on the road of religion. We have unbounded faith in God, and that while we implicitly trust in Him we can never go religiously wrong.

WHAT IS SPACE ?

Space is boundless and eternal. It is a sea without limit, without shores. In it all things swim and float. Without space no real existence is possible, and it is only as things occupy different positions of space that we can distinguish one from another. Space is, and must of necessity be, infinite. We may cast our minds thousands of miles and billions of leagues away, but imagination is compelled to stop, tired with its flight. Let it again take flight billions of billions of leagues, and we find some impediment to its flight. What is that impediment ? Is it a solid substance ? How far does that stretch onward ? Does it end ? What then is beyond that ? The mind is wearied—it returns to itself and asserts that there can be no boundary to space, above, below, to the right, to the left ; in any and in every direction it stretches on for ever and for ever. Comprehend this we cannot, believe it we must. Wherever we go, whether in body or mind, eternal space and its twin brother time are our companions. The one is the illimitable ocean, the other is the illimitable atmosphere, that are below, above, and everywhere surrounding us.

WHAT IS SCIENCE ?

It is a common thing for people to use the word Science without having any definite knowledge of what it means. In brief it is only another word for knowledge. When this knowledge is classified and directed to some particular end, then we give that science a name. Thus we have the science of Botany, of

Astronomy, of Conchology, and so forth. John Stuart Mill says: "The language of science is, this is so, and this is not so. Science observes phenomena, and endeavors to discover their law." Professor Huxley says: "True science and true religion are twin sisters, and the separation of either from the other is sure to prove the death of both. Science prospers exactly in proportion as it is religious, and religion flourishes in exact proportion to the scientific depth and firmness of its basis. The great deeds of philosophers have been less the fruit of their intellect than of the direction of that intellect by an eminently religious state of mind. Truth has yielded herself rather to their patience, their love, their single heartedness, and their self-denial, than to their logical acumen." In corroboration of this view we instance the science of metaphysical healing as also a religion, or, to speak more definitely, it is a branch of religion. When some persons hear of cures by the mental treatment, they ask: "But do you use any scientific methods?" We answer: "This is a science, and though its phenomena are not so well known and classified as in the case of some other sciences, it is nevertheless none the less a science on that account. As a science, it has effected cures where other scientific methods have failed."

www.ingramcontent.com/pod-product-compliance
Lightning Source LLC
Chambersburg PA
CBHW020231030726
47497CB00009B/3042